Weeping Tomato

by

Samantha Rumbidzai Vazhure

First published in Great Britain in 2024 by:

Carnelian Heart Publishing Ltd
Suite A
82 James Carter Road
Mildenhall
Suffolk
IP28 7DE
UK

www.carnelianheartpublishing.co.uk

Paperback ISBN   978-1-914287-71-8
Hardback ISBN   978-1-914287-72-5
eBook ISBN   978-1-914287-73-2

A CIP catalogue record for this book is available from the British Library.

Editors: Panashe Lazarus Nyagwambo & Innocent Whande

Cover art & interior artworks: Mike Stuart

Typeset by Carnelian Heart Publishing Ltd
Layout and formatting by DanTs Media

To those

who have reclaimed,

who are seeking &

who will seek

to reclaim their freedom &

journey back to the truth.

Contents

"The whole universe is contained within a single human being—you. Everything that you see around, including the things you might not be fond of and even the people you despise or abhor, is present within you in varying degrees. Therefore, do not look for Sheitan outside yourself either. The devil is not an extraordinary force that attacks from without. It is an ordinary voice within. If you get to know yourself fully, facing with honesty and hardness both your dark and bright sides, you will arrive at a supreme form of consciousness. When a person knows himself or herself, he or she knows God."

~Elif Shafak, The Forty Rules of Love

Prologue

You want to go home, *but where is your home?*

Where the heart is, your ego might say.

But where is the heart? the voice of truth asks.

The year is 2090-something, maybe.

The glimmering panorama is speckled with lucent diamonds and dark kimberlite hues. Deep blue sapphires are layered with violet amethysts like bluebells shrouding distant rolling hills, and the air carries a sweet scent of springtime blossoms. Baby-blue aquamarines fused with emeralds into yellowish beryl clusters, like small, dotted daisies, contrast gracefully with translucent pink and purple-red garnets cuddled beneath an unblemished lazuline sky. The fiery-orange marigolds and crimson tulips are in fact lustrous deep-red rubies, native gold rocks, and burnt-orange carnelians nestled between the cleavages of royal-green emerald boulders like jewels hidden in plain sight. Except here, there are no lustful eyes yearning. Yellow citrines, pearlescent opals, sparkling blue topaz - charming like buttercups, dandelions and forget me nots. A multitude of variegated agates exude otherworldly energies, curing sick flesh and minds before carriers of disease become aware of their afflictions.

As the large yellow sun casts its golden glow to light up the majestic world beneath you, it feels like basking in the warmth of cherished moments where time slows down, and every shade and sparkle triggers captured memories, like finding forgotten treasure in an old chest. Like uncovering a sweet truth.

Akin to a vibrant tapestry of wildflowers in perpetual propagation, erupting, augmenting, like sweet-coloured-popcorn, the soothing clatter of rolling pebbles sharpens your gaze.

The Mutirikwi valley is littered with iridescent precious stones, the shit of cyborg lions. Mhondo-bots are bionic animals programmed by Dzim-AI to consume anything vile and improper. Dzim-AI takes instructions only from the voice of Mwari, heard when a ratified SaNgoma beats the sacred drum, Ngoma Inoti Ngundu!

The air is clean, and so are the well-fed people of Dzimbabgwe. The kingdom is wealthy, joyous and proper. Only good things happen here, and this is where the heart is.

You've arrived on a chartered private jet to pay your last respects to Mudavose, who held onto life until the ripe age of 118.

Garisanai, your guide, is your older cousin, a woman in her mid-60s. She collects you from the airport and chaperones you to the fortress in a solar-powered, self-flying car. She appears calm and regal, her long dreadlocked hair, neck and wrists adorned with multi-coloured seed beads and polished cowrie shells, *ndoro chena*. You can't help noticing the contrast with your hoody, jeans and trainers you've arrived wearing from England.

Gari, as she likes to be called, carries an intricately carved *mutovhoti* stick to repel negative energies. After exchanging pleasantries, she withdraws a small *nhekwe* from the side pocket of her vibrant motif-embossed kaftan and offers you *bute rematare*. She pours a small heap of the earthy powder into your palm before demonstrating how to pull in the snuff. You sniff it a few times like you've done it before, and immediately, you feel like you're perched beneath a gentle drizzle of lotus flower petals. As your tensions and anxieties dissipate, Gari smiles victoriously then begins a running commentary of the scenery below.

"On our right are the Mutirikwi research and STEM centres built over the years with solid agate bricks, using a similar design concept to the Great Zimbabwe Monument – do you see the chevron patterns at the top of the dentelle-layered stones?"

"Yes!" you say, remembering when you learnt on some BBC documentary, that the patterns symbolised fertility in women. "They symbolise continuity in generations, don't they!"

"Ahum. And these buildings are home to some of the world-leading scientists, mathematicians, physicists, and biologists who returned home from the diaspora to be part of the Dzimbabgwe rebuild. It is where the most cutting-edge research is carried out. Our scientists were the first to invent the cure for AIDS and other endemics, which we now export globally…Check out those Mhondo-bots ahead of us!" By the time you look, they are gone.

"They're one of our many inventions. With heads of *mhondoro,* or lions as you'd call them, Mhondo-bots have razor-sharp intuition and robotic bodies; the beasts are indestructible! You rarely see them, but they smell trouble and sense intrusions of any ill-intended visits from hundreds of miles away and devour adversaries with no warning. Their proficiency is evidenced by the precious landscape you see around us…piles and piles of excess from the corrupt people who lived before us, and those who tried to re-colonise the people of this land. This wealth belongs to the people of Dzimbabgwe. All of them! No one here goes without." Garisanai gestures dramatically, with gratification, remembering how Mudavose's inaugural speech had been narrated to her by her own parents.

"We can never have upright rulers if society is breeding and nurturing corrupt children. We will forever harvest rotten fruit if we do not sincerely change our ways. Let us look inward and cleanse whatever is foul within us, to raise a generation that might contribute positively to society. If the process of cleansing the muck amongst us is effective, we can self-govern. Allow me to unveil the latest invention from Mutirikwi Research Centre – 5000 Mhondo-bots. These new enforcement officers will employ a uniform standard to maintain peace and harmony in our land. Using the latest technology and AI programmed by the voice of Mwari via Ngoma Inoti Ngundu, there will be no more corruption and self-serving practices to advantage a select few while the masses suffer. We are all equal in the eyes of Mwari, and so it shall be in the kingdom of Dzimbabgwe!" The masses had cheered and as they were celebrating the new order of the day, army tanks had appeared from nowhere, ready to destroy Mudavose and her followers. The Mhondo-bots, each with the agility of 1000 horses, had immediately pounced towards the

daring humans and their artillery, tearing it all apart,
devouring the relics like industrial vacuum cleaners and
immediately defecating precious stones. And Dzimbabgwe
had been wealthy and prosperous since then.

Now a middle-aged woman, Garisanai has witnessed the developments she's reciting, since childhood.

"That's impressive! I knew this place would be special, but as you know, there's no media coverage of it, and so I had no idea! I wish I'd come sooner…" you tell Garisanai.

"Well, better late than never. Keeping the treasures of Dzimbabgwe secret helps to ensure we don't attract the wrong audience. We never want to be colonised again! On the left, over there," Garisanai points to a vast area covered with photovoltaics perched beneath a consistently hot sun. "That is our solar farm. 30,000 square kilometres of those solar panels generate more than enough electricity for Dzimbabgwe, and we export the rest to wherever it's needed."

"Wow!"

"It had to be done. I mean, I was a late teen when it all started, but I do remember the loadshedding back in the day. Sometimes we went to school hungry because there was no way to cook a decent meal with no electricity. Firewood was scarce due to deforestation. Back then, Zhingoz arrived from all directions to chop down trees without replacing them. Their only focus was to blast granite, displacing our people without compensating them. And stupid officials bribed with pittances allowed it. Anyway, I digress… I don't know why no one came up with such an obvious idea before. Solar farms are perfect because we have so much land and so much sun!"

"You know how the saying goes, Gari. Common sense is not common." You have already decided, you're never leaving this place.

As you get closer to the fortress, fields of lush-green maize and many varieties of fruit and crops sandwich the road, occasionally punctuated beautifully by miombo vegetation. You arrive at the border post where

Garisanai lowers the vehicle, looks into a camera and large iron gates open for the flying car to enter.

***

Mudavose's funeral is a farewell festivity attended by countless officials from everywhere. Early morning, as the sun is rising, the celebration begins, for a revolution of collective responsibility instilled by a woman who brought back the voluntary cooperation of society to achieve love, peace, and harmony that had been absent for centuries. The wise counsel is made up of two women and a man who step up to the podium to honour Mudavose.

"Mudavose and the team of leading scientists managed to eradicate numerous diseases that had been consuming the people of this land alive. The people had felt like they were being punished for lifetimes of unforgivable sins, burning in a hell here on earth, and she brought water with her, all the way from Mabgweadziva, to put out the fire that was consuming us alive. She arrived at a crucial time when our natural resources were at great risk. Forces from the East were stripping our land of its wealth while the ordinary citizen suffered a lack of bare provisions. She brought back the fundamentals of traditional African society – absence of classes and gender inequality, or authoritative structures, just the voice of Mwari leading us all as equal human beings." Mbgwanhema then nods at Mbiziyegono to take over as she descends the podium.

"On the day she arrived from Matonjeni, she followed Mwari's instructions to heal our kingdom in just six days! On the seventh day, *chisi*, she rested before embarking on her life-long journey of maintaining peace and generating prosperity in this beautiful kingdom. And she did a marvellous job! Now, it is good that her closest surviving relative is here today, because we the wise counsel have read Mudavose's will, which decrees her granddaughter, Murenga, her successor as custodian of Ngoma Inoti Ngundu! Her inauguration will be held in a month's time, after a rigorous induction programme in a sacred place that is known only to the wise counsel."

Gasps of delight grace the air as Mbiziyegono bows, nods at Moyomurefu, and descends the podium. Mbiziyegono is dark, tall, and strong, occasionally stealing glances at you. You sense his interest, and in another lifetime it might have triggered your fervency, but you serve him apathy instead. However, you're surprised by his announcement and grateful for being the chosen one.

"To ensure a seamless passing of our *gwendengwe*, may we peacefully pay our last respects to the revered Mudavose," Moyomurefu instructs, as she descends towards the selenite casket, shortly to be carried into a cave beneath the fortress for the final private rituals. Six women lift Mudavose's body, with you in attendance to witness the *chivanhu* burial rites of your beloved. Inside the cave, the casket remains uncovered, and Mudavose's embalmed body is turned sideways to fulfil her wish – to sleep comfortably on her right side, forever.

A passage to facilitate the exit of Mudavose's spirit, should she wish to exit the grave as a *mhondoro*, is arranged. A long hollow reed is placed next to Mudavose's ear, leading to the entrance of the cave. A leaf is placed at the open end of the reed, and should it be blown off the following night, the spirit of Mudavose will reveal itself as a *mhondoro*.

The tomb is sealed by a large boulder, leaving a tiny aperture for the reed-end and leaf to stick out. Mudavose's place of rest is guarded in perpetuity by Mhondo-bots. At its entrance, installations of majestic soapstone carvings of *hungwe* and *chapungu* perch on either side of the vault access, both with humanlike facial features. Gigantic serpentine sculptures of Nehanda Charwe Nyakasikana and Kaguvi Gumboreshumba stand next to the birds. In their eyes are CCTV cameras linked to the Mhondo-bots and the research centre that monitors suspicious movement around the tomb.

Two days later, a young, pale maneless lion is seen wandering at the entrance of the tomb before disappearing into nearby bushes. The CCTV monitors can see that the leaf at the reed-end is gone.

You're dropped off at the sandy shore of Lake Mutirikwi by Garisanai to meet an undisclosed mentor for your new role.

At first, like a dung ball rolling ahead of a lethargic beetle, it is neither momentous nor exciting. It soon transforms into a dusty cloud in orbital motion, becoming more and more rancorous as it looms. As the large cone-shaped mass of dust approaches, your gut responds with excitement. The whirlwind advances at inordinate speed and scoops you off the ground, carrying you to a dimension parallel to ours. Inside the dusty spectacle is a lake called Dzivaguru, larger than Mutirikwi.

A mesmerising creature emerges from the water and introduces itself as Dananai. Its upper body is of a woman with eyes as dazzling as the Dzimbabgwe landscape, inundated with precious stones. You're not fazed by the paleness of Dananai, but it is the bottom part of her body that throws you off when she rises above the water to reveal a shimmering motley of variegated scales. She is the most beautiful thing you have ever seen! Her hair resembles the rich red soil of Dzimbabgwe and is bunched into several long kinky knots of *mhotsi* which fall over her bust to clothe her breasts. Her body is covered with silky strands of hair, and her arms are long and strong, with fins in her armpits and webs between her fingers. Sometimes, her fins expand in glorious motion and open gracefully wide like the bloom of a nocturnal cactus.

Dananai's beauty cannot be described by earthly language. On her spine is a larger dorsal fin that beats faster than canary wings. When she beckons, you swim towards her and latch onto her back. You hold onto her neck for support as she rises above the water to show off her charming calico of scales.

Dananai takes off to give you a tour of her domain, vast and backdropped by hills and roaring rivers, waterfalls with rainbows in nameless hues. There, suns and moons illume their light continuously, and all galaxies and their stars are beautifully brazen.

Back on the shore of Dzivaguru, she gazes into the core of your eyes, beaming with love and joy.

"How wonderful it is to see you, Murenga. Welcome to Mugomba!"

"Thank you." You smile in awe.

"Murenga… do you accept the responsibility we are about to bestow on you?"

"My grandmother's legacy is evident in Dzimbabgwe. Keeping it alive would be the greatest honour."

"That is precisely what I wanted to hear. Unlike the SaNgomas who are born with the earthly gift to beat sacred drums on behalf of their ancestors, you are a KaNgoma! A deity incarnate that comes bearing different principalities of light. Your drum is inward and you dance to your own tune." Dananai smiles wistfully and goes on to say, "In this lifetime, have you yet seen a crocodile?"

"I saw an alligator at a Florida beach once…"

"Well, comparing an alligator to a crocodile is like comparing a pussycat to a lion. The latter is larger and more aggressive, elusive, and difficult to catch if you manage to capture it before it does you. And more importantly, an alligator bite weighs in at around 2500 pounds per square inch, whereas a crocodile's is about 3,800. Crocodiles have the strongest jaws amongst all animals placed on Earth by Mwari. Do you see where I'm going with this?"

"Ohh-kayy!" Fear and doubt begin to trickle into your consciousness.

"According to *chivanhu*, a crocodile is connected to sacred pools where *njuzu* spirits reside. Dzivaguru is one such place. At your inauguration, in accordance with ancient Karanga tradition, you must catch and kill a crocodile from Mutirikwi, to symbolise that you have the strength and connection to the founding spirits of Dzimbabgwe. Your triumph will be celebrated with a sacred meal cooked with gemstones retrieved from the crocodile's stomach." Dananai explains.

"You sound certain that I'll succeed…I'm the most unfit human being you'll ever come across…plus I can't swim!"

"Rid your ego and remove any doubt from your psyche, dear Murenga! Your purpose on earth is to change narratives and create new systems that are aligned with the code of cosmic powers, the laws of the universe. Just like Mudavose, you rebirthed yourself, so you have the strength to achieve what other beings cannot. From today going forth, I will train you daily the way I taught Mudavose. Like you, Mudavose came to me with no experience of fighting, but I made her fight beasts 100 times stronger than the strongest ones on earth, and when the time came, she fought a most notorious crocodile that had wreaked havoc among the people of Dzimbabgwe. Mudavose ground that beast to mince before it was cooked. Its body is the one carved on one side of the *hakata* used by SaNgoma commissioned to beat Ngoma Inoti Ngundu today. Mudavose's face is carved on the parallel side to represent the competing life forces in this world. And you too will conquer the same way Mudavose did, and your face will replace hers on the new *hakata*. Let the rhythm of your inward drum beat to awaken the precious KaNgoma in you!"

Part one

Weeping Tomato

James and I are penguins, loyal to each other no matter what. We met at the University of Birmingham when he was completing his MBA and I, a freshman, fell for the tall, muscular, handsome Korekore man. Cliché, but true.

We got married immediately following my graduation. "Till death do us part" was our life goal, though James has done a fair bit of roaming around, especially in his youth, but always remembering to come home to keep me sweet. Initially, his generosity and gentleness surpassed his marital misdemeanours, until I got tired of his shady ways, and each incident began chipping away at my heart until there was nothing left.

Although I was tempted to leave, I found life too hectic to accommodate the onerous admin of divorce. Looking after James, three children and trying to break through tough career ceilings kept my hands full, so I kept going, barely noticing the gradual voiding in my chest.

Now in my late-forties, life suddenly feels like burnt butterless toast – bitter and unswallowable, and at best, bland, like I am doing nothing more than waiting for death. What I find most disturbing is my emotional numbness. I do not remember the last time I wept or laughed. Sometimes I feel like a repressive cork is stuck in my throat, keeping my fizz imperceptible like bottled vintage champagne, its explosion preserved for a worthy call.

Vimbai and John, our first-born twins, are in their final year at Bath University, and our lastborn, Peter, is a year away from writing his A Level exams at St. Dubitrius. He has a girlfriend now, and she seems to have diverted all of his attention from me. When the last chick flies from my nest, what will become of me?

James spends his free time mentoring and grooming Peter for life when he is not away consulting with large corporations in London or playing golf at the Celtic Manor.

When the twins completed their private schooling and left for university, we paid off our mortgage and James encouraged me to work part time so I could do more nesting, gardening, hanging out with his friends' wives, amongst other such mundane things. Since the Covid-19 pandemic, I've been working remotely as a part-time managing consultant for start-up tech companies.

Our imposing six-bedroom house sits on a five-acre estate in rural Herefordshire and feels like a ghost town. When I'm not reading African literature, I'm on social media seeking human connection. I've made a few online friends who share some of my passions. I feel drawn to content on writing and visual art, and I've become a part of those communities. I'm also engrossed with fighting for women empowerment and the rights of underrepresented groups.

None of our children speak my mother tongue. James and I speak to them in English although we converse with each other in chiShona sometimes. I yearn for a deep, meaningful nexus, for conversations in chiShona, and I miss Zimbabwe, but we haven't been there for a good eight years.

When Zimbabweans dotted all over the world follow me on social media, I follow back those who don't share noxious content. I spend a considerable amount of my free time on Twitter, now called X but that name will never catch on; occasionally posting my spiritual think pieces and pictures of myself swimming in the streams or rambling in the woodlands near our home. It's difficult to judge if I'm over-sharing, so I'm cautious in the curation of my social media posts, keeping my views as neutral as possible, and my personal life as private as possible.

I find the Afro Bloggers handle wholesome and I'm part of their community, which has inspired me to start a poetry blog where I record random musings about life as a writer. Each Wednesday, I participate in their poetry prompts, which they share to their thousands of followers, and that has grown my following significantly. Discussing my writing on social media has become a huge part of my life, and I aspire to write my own book one day.

An avatar has been appearing in my dreams, each time intonating my most revered lines of poetry by Mary Oliver:

> *You do not have to be good*
> *You do not have to walk on your knees*
> *For a hundred miles through the desert, repenting.*
> *You only have to let the soft animal of your body love what it loves.*

The avatar disappears, leaving only his honeyed recital to rock me out of slumber. I desperately long for my dreams to prolong so I can engage him, but they are as brief and measured as the verse itself. My mysterious encounters with him are as delicious as visitations by Vishnu, emerging from nowhere like autumn mist to love me in my sleep. It seems the more I give thought and weight to my visions, the more persistent they become, like vicious sleet pelting sideways on a windy winter's day.

My latest visitation from the avatar coincides with menopausal insomnia, after which I quake from the vivid dream, drenched in sweat, and pick up my phone to inspect it for bad news, as one does when they're unceremoniously roused. I find instead, a soothing surprise.

Adam, one of my social media followers, regularly likes my pictures and poems, sometimes commenting on my posts, but I've thought nothing of it until now, when I open his direct message on Twitter. I notice for the first time that his profile picture strongly resembles the avatar in my dreams.

"Hello, my sister. I just wanted to say how much I enjoy your posts. I'm from Masvingo like you. Perhaps, when you have time, we could chat on WhatsApp?"

"Hi my brother, of course! Good to know *muri wezhira*. Let me share my number and we can speak when it's mutually convenient."

We exchange phone numbers and hit it off immediately, like long-lost twins, sending each other messages every waking moment. Within a week, Adam knows everything there is to know about my mundane, shielded life. I do not find it strange to open up to a stranger, but what I find strange is his lack of judgement on my strange life.

He says he's self-employed and works in construction, in Johannesburg. He lives in Yeoville and grew up in Mucheke, the biggest ghetto in Masvingo, and he is ever so proud of his roots.

"We lived at Pangolin, and I did my grade one and two at Vurombo, then three to seven at Don Bosco. I did my secondary *pa*Ndarama, A-level at Gokomere, then Civil Engineering *pa*Masvingo Tech. You see, I'm born and bred there!"

He also tells me he hates organised religion, capitalism, colonialism and social injustices I've never really paid attention to, because I've never needed to.

I was raised in the more affluent, low density Rhodene, where the most colourful happening was jacarandas in bloom. I attended Victoria Junior boarding school in Masvingo, then Midlands Christian College in Gweru where I received private secondary education. Thereafter I was accepted at Birmingham University in the UK, for a BSc in International Business.

Having grown up in the church, I am demure, obedient and faithful in all my doings, but now, especially with social media influencing, I've gradually become curious about rebellion and freedom.

Adam notices the little things. The things I like and those I don't, piquing every word said and not said. I've learnt to tread carefully to avoid offending him, as that is what usually happens when one is privileged, and the other is not. He seems lovely and I don't want to jeopardise our friendship. I want to understand him.

Eventually, Adam says he wonders what my voice sounds like and asks if we can speak. Curious to meet my avatar, I ask if he wants to video call, and he agrees.

James is away for a week on business, so I arrange a virtual meeting with Adam one evening after work. I feed and water Peter first, and he traipses off to bed early, exhausted with rugby practice.

When Adam's face appears on the screen after a few minutes of internet connection troubles, he is blushing. His dark face has a few premature folds and wrinkles that tell a story of…lack? This does not bother me. In fact, it draws me to him more. I can tell he's younger than me but can't guess his age. I like that his age is not obvious.

"Wow Zorodzai, you're glowing. And you look more beautiful right now than in any of the pictures of yours I've seen online. I wish I could smell your skin." I'm taken aback by his directness.

"You don't really mean that, do you? Thank you," I blush too, completely disoriented by his compliment. I don't remember the last time any man expressed their appreciation of my physical beauty. It somewhat feels like a mockery and my face betrays me.

"Why do you find it difficult to accept the truth? You should embrace the things the universe sends your way, and it will give you more."

"You should write poetry!" I can't help but laugh.

"Maybe I should. I love reading the poems you post on social media. In fact, I look forward to reading them. Everyday. You write beautifully." His voice is husky but velvety, portraying a vulnerability that makes me want to save him from whatever is tormenting him. He tells me that he often feels empty inside, and that he thinks about dying, a lot. I confide in him, that I too have experienced what he is going through and promise to write him a poem one of these days.

As our call progresses, I notice that Adam has a thick, discoloured unkempt afro, left to lock naturally. In my thoughts, I can't resist tugging and measuring a strand of it—it must be at least 20 centimetres long. Every so often, he smiles broadly, revealing a perfectly even set of white teeth that makes me think he must be a good kisser. I should be embarrassed by such thoughts, but the more I try to tame them, the more rebellious they become.

We speak for six hours with no breaks, and I come off the call reborn and swollen with want.

Adam has ignited feelings I thought had long died with my youth. For days following our video call, I feel young and sexy again and can't stop thinking about him.

When James is home, he carries on with the busyness of his world, while I bask in the glory of my new friendship with Adam. I think it's too late to tell James about Adam, not without giving away the truth of how he really makes me feel. Since the night we spoke, I think and write in verse. Sometimes I write poems on my phone, sometimes on my laptop, sometimes I handwrite them in my journal and read them out loud. I have immeasurable creative energy flowing through me and the writer's block that sometimes plagues me is now a thing of the past.

HONEY

Having wandered deep dark forests, where
fallen leaves lie still with hints of sweet decay
Where shadows weave through trees and
light spills onto gentle-flowing streams
With endless hoping for true love to take root
amid the embrace of life and death
I catch the whiff of raw honey, with
flavours and tones so intense, to heal my ailing heart
Oh honey, shall I start a fire to chase the bees away so
I can make you mine?

I cannot believe how Adam has affected me enough to override my resolution to be faithful to James. But I press *send* and wait anxiously for his response. Adam does not respond till the next day. First, he apologises and explains there was no electricity in Johannesburg, and that his phone had run out of charge.

"Wow! Zorodzai? Wow, I'm overawed! I read & reread it & it got better every time. The gracefulness of your imagery is truly moving. I'm so grateful for our connection. I'm truly moved."

My heart nearly orgasms when I read his reply. For the first time since we started interacting, I long to be in his physical presence. As if by telepathy, the message I knew would eventually come arrives.

"Don't reign yourself in. It's not worth it. We have one life to live and it's not usually the case that we get a chance to be young again. Zorodzai, let's be young again and live in our secret kingdom where only you and I exist."

"But Adam, I'm nearly 50. And I have a husband and three children."

"Zorodzai, that poem you wrote was the seismic bomb that turned my world upside down. I'm 35 and don't care how old you are, or who else is in your life. I want to be a part of you. I want to worship you, show you what real love is."

"Why are you this wonderful, yet single?"

"Being good to people doesn't guarantee that they'll be good to you. I've been let down so many times and I've rather enjoyed the peace of being on my own."

"Care to share what happened?"

"I don't talk about my exes. All my breakups were mutual, and I respect my exes as human beings. I've actually stayed friends with them."

"You've remained friends with people who let you down?"

"I don't hold grudges *ini*."

"Fair enough. Well, you do know that we might never meet, right?" I say to Adam, but really, I'm affirming to myself the safety of an online affair. What could possibly go wrong when we're so far apart?

"I know. Let us enjoy each other in the moment and take each day as it comes."

I immediately fall in love with the idea of love with no intention of further commitment. To just love, exploring and savouring the feeling, observing it and doing nothing about it. This is the sort of brain-altering, electrifying romance I've been longing for, and it sets my soul on fire. His words melt my core into an oozing chocolate fondant. "Yes, let's do it. Me and you in our own little kingdom."

And just like that, what I thought had been a life to be proud of becomes meaningless, painful even. Money and comfort seem worthless to me, stupid even. All I want is Adam. He tells me he loves me many times a day, and his "I love you's" don't just come in three letter words. They are florid, sapid and palliative, and when he says it in Shona, my heart simply explodes.

NDINOKUDA

Love avowals may come swathed
in ribbons of shimmering silk,
stored in crystal ewers
or in rare ethnic pottery—
But love only seeps into my veins
when engraved in the poetry
of my mother's tongue…
Ndinokuda

As my world turns and spins, I constantly remind myself that I'm ready to receive this love, and offer it to God in prayer:

Mwari baba,
Please help me to accept this love fully without self-sabotaging.
May I remember every day to lean into the joy of love,
and that I deserve to be loved.
I deserve this!
Amen.

I'm in a state of constant euphoria, and Adam's indulgent utterances make him the perfect muse for my poems. I especially get excited by his raunchy morning text messages.

"Call me before you pee."

"Babe! Why?"

"I want to hear the precious trickle of your divine feminine waters flowing into the toilet chamber. I'm at work, so I won't speak. Just call and wee, ok?"

I love a delicious start to my day. I jump out of bed and call him, aiming for the toilet water so as to urinate loudly to ensure he hears it all the way in Johannesburg. I can hear him breathing heavily with helpless desire. I giggle and hang up.

"That was beautiful, my love." He texts immediately. "In the absence of physical contact, that is the closest I can get to making love to you. Do you know how sacred your pussy is? Anything that passes through it is special too. The first urine of the day is ancient medicine used in our village to heal fresh wounds to this day. I want to drink your urine so it can heal my soul."

I can't believe his words. Moreso because James is vaguely interested in any of my body fluids and has nothing exciting to say about my body. We barely touch, and we have one monthly bout of dry sex. I often wonder if he sets a calendar reminder to do it, because it always happens around the same time of the month. That's how it's been for years; it is as routine as taking his suits to the drycleaners. I drive there absent-minded and feel nothing about the tedium. I've been uninterested in sex and never think about it… until now.

Before we know it, Adam and I are exchanging provocative images of each other. At first, he's queuing up for something in town when he shares a picture of his hung protuberance, and from our serene, manicured garden, I reply with braless swollen nipples covered by a threadbare muddy vest. In only a matter of days, nude photographs of each other are flying between South Africa and England. Seeing his sculpted body… his standing thing makes me want to sprint to him across sea and land. He says he never works out, but he looks lean and palatable.

Sometimes I stand in front of the mirror, shaping and reshaping my mouth around the phantom of his manhood, like a fish ingesting water for oxygen. I reconstruct his voice in my head to form grunts and squeals of pleasure, and this only exacerbates my appetite for him.

"Oh my, your breasts! They don't look like they were ever suckled. Are you sure you have three children?"

"Yes, my darling, I breastfed two boys and a girl!"

"*Eish*, I can't wait to suck them. I want to squeeze them hard and fuck your cleavage. You know, I can go for hours, *fanika nezvawakaita iwewe so, handitundi!* You have no idea what I'm going to do to you when I see you."

"You're winding me up Adam. Should the opposite not be true, that if I'm sexy you'll ejaculate quicker…?"

"Noooo! That's fake science. I can do you all night long, especially when I'm drunk."

"You're nuts…"

"*Nokuti gare gare tofa, saka kana ndodhla imbwa, ndododhla iri honho, kana zviri zvimbwanana ndoodhla zviri* two two!"

I cackle at his ghetto remix of our Shona proverb. When I laugh with him, the tension in my belly melts away, evaporating like the heat of my menopausal flashes.

"When we meet, I'm going to buy cheese for the match."

"What do you mean?" I'm excited that he has said "when" and not "if".

"I mean I will actually buy cheese and eat it as an aphrodisiac. You know a sexual encounter is called a 'match', right?" I love learning his ghetto lingo, and our dirty talk turns me on every day. With my vagina ever misty, my body begins to demand what it can't have.

Sometimes, Adam and I share random pictures of boring things to dilute the crassness prevailing in our relationship. Little life niggles, like when my big toe is pricked whilst gardening barefooted and I send him a picture of my injury. He says he wishes he could "pull out the prick and kiss it better" and I'm besotted with his devotion.

i'll take a lover who zooms in on every one of my pictures &
says a poem for each of my bumps, scars, lines & curves;

he'll sing a song for each hair on my skin, both wanted &
unwanted till it knows its place;

foretells when next i'll laugh or cry just by looking
at my eyes' corners to count their crinkles;

decipher the depth of my delight by calculating
the projection of my skyward lips;

hate the cinch of my clothes & yearn to rip them off
to unleash my flesh into his ravenous hands;

& spot the thorn splinter on my hallux, pull it out
with tenderness that puts me out like his phallus.

When James gets home, he peers over my shoulder to make out what's on my laptop screen.

"You're glowing," his compliment sounds more like a question. "What are you writing these days?"

I show him 'Lover's Couplet' and he throws his head back to release the loudest taunting belly laugh, his broad shoulders dancing to the rhythm of his amusement.

"*Zvinoitika kupiko izvi?*" He questions my delusion when composure eventually finds him.

"There are men out there who can love this way!" My eyes roll after him screaming, *you have no idea!*

"Show me one and I'll give you a thousand bucks!" He walks off, his instruction trailing him, "Make us a cuppa, will you…with cream teas to go with!" I can magic tea scones in half an hour, so I oblige him.

I rub in cold butter to sifted rice flour with organic wholegrain spelt to give the scones a crunchy texture. I add a pinch of Himalayan pink salt, a spoonful of coconut sugar and a cupful of lime-soaked craisins before mixing in some oat milk mixed with buttermilk, kneading and cutting up the dough which I glaze with duck egg. I place the scones on a baking tray in my hot Aga and put the kettle on.

The sweet, buttery aroma of freshly baked scones wafts in the air. There's homemade strawberry preserve with fruit from our own vines.

I serve the cream teas with my delicious jam and dollops of luxuriously light, velvety mascarpone instead of the traditional Cornish clotted cream, which is denser and higher in fat content.

"No more than two for you *hantika!* Gotta keep that shit tight..." *Mscheeeew!* I'm surprised that James playfully slaps my buttocks as I walk off – something he hasn't done in years.

At night, I douse myself in sensual oils and hook my legs around James's legs to draw him in, and this shocks him at first, but he begins to comply. When I wheedle, he turns to face me. Without bothering with foreplay, James climbs and pounds me unforgivingly, as quickly as he can, grunting in delight that I'm so wet, then disembarks after relieving himself, faces the other way and immediately snores. Left seething with unsatiated desire, I begin to think of other ways to quench my thirst for Adam.

I search online for sex toys and find a silicone dildo that resembles Adam's member. James feels moribund, and at best insipid, like an over-refrigerated avocado. I hate that he won't make me orgasm like he used to. I'm ecstatic when my new toy arrives, but after two or three sessions, it begins to feel cold and tasteless, like James's penis, and all I want is to be with the source of my longing.

I order a thick rose quartz crystal wand, and I'm so excited for it, it needs a name. At first I think Abraham, because it rhymes with Adam. Then my mind takes me back to *Abrahama weJudhiya* in my childhood Christmas plays. 'Abraham of Judah' sounds like a cool name, but it's too long to moan out loud when I play with myself. I find myself on Google searching for a reminder of the story – turns out the tribe of Judah got its name from a descendant of Abraham called Judah. *Let's go with that then*. Judah. It's less conspicuous and as unassuming as Adam.

Judah is delicious, but again, after a few uses, I find it is not as therapeutic as I had hoped. Only Adam can really put out the fire raging between my thighs.

As our love flourishes, I think of ways Adam and I could be together, until one day I suggest, "Why don't we meet?"

"Where? How?"

"We could meet somewhere neutral. A holiday resort perhaps?"

"And what would you tell your husband?"

"We probably need to brainstorm that together."

After a few days of deliberating, we come up with the perfect plan. To meet in Victoria Falls. I will tell James I'm going for a girls' reunion with my high school friends. A week is all I need. If we survive that week together, I'll come back home to pack my bags and divorce James. I want to be loved deeply for the rest of my days.

"What are you doing right now?"

"I'm loading the washing machine. Then I've got to fill the dishwasher…"

"Why do you seem to be the only one who slaves around that house?"

"They just won't help me…"

"Leave it then. Let them run out of clothes to wear and let's see if they don't remember how to wash their own clothes. Don't do those dishes. When they run out of clean cups and plates, they'll know what to do. Listen to me… don't cook tonight. Order yourself some takeaway and go straight to bed after eating. When they get home to an empty kitchen, they'll know what to do."

Now heedless to any good that ever came out of my marriage, I suddenly feel angry at how mediocre my life has been for three whole decades with James.

How could I allow one man to sap my soul like this? My whole life has been centred around making him feel like a king. Cooking, cleaning, mothering him and his children. To what end? I don't even know whether he loves me. I have no life, except the bit of gardening and writing I do to pass time on social media. And now, this young, handsome, clever man sees the beauty in me and has the energy to tell me, daily, how special I am. My life feels worth living again.

With such thoughts brewing in my head daily, it's not difficult to convince James about my high school reunion. The man is barely interested in any of my escapades. I book my flight and begin to prepare to meet the love of my life.

We're meeting in six weeks' time. I begin to exercise and eat less, and when I laugh at myself in our messages, explaining to Adam that I can't remember the last time I tried to flatten my stomach for a man, he says, "My dear Zoro, why on earth would you put yourself through that? You are perfect the way you are. In fact, I would prefer it if you were larger. A big African woman is my type of woman."

I immediately quit dieting and begin to eat and drink what I want, much to James's annoyance. James has always wanted a presentable trophy wife and has something to say about everything I put in my mouth, going as far as finding my empty packets of junk food in the bin to calculate the calories for me. In fact, most times when I get James's attention, it's to do with how much I'm eating and the weight I'm putting on. Or telling-off for buying full-fat and sugary versions of foods that have low-fat or *no sugar added* varieties – mayonnaise, yoghurt, milk, soft drinks and such.

As Adam and I converse daily, he barely speaks about travelling to Victoria Falls.

"How will you get there?" I want to know if he can afford it. I will pay for his flight if he needs me to, but I'm too embarrassed to make the offer.

"I'm still trying to work out a route, see my options, you know. I might get a bus that goes via Botswana…"

"A bus! I don't want you getting there tired. Surely you can find cheap flights… I can help you look?" Having lost all reason, I feel stupidly happy. *How is it possible to feel this much love at my age?*

"Don't worry, sweetness. I'll be there." I worry that he won't. I send him a poem I've been reworking for weeks, to fan our fire.

~~*FALLING*~~

~~*Love shots pump into my aorta*~~
~~*bursts of euphoric hormones*~~
~~*inducing copious marbling to my tenderloin*~~
~~*like a Matsusaka wagyu cow*~~
~~*massaged throughout its life by a geisha boy*~~
~~*and tickled to its death by the tail feather of an albatross*~~
~~*only to end up a Chateaubriand*~~
~~*devoured at full tilt by a half-arsed magnate*~~

~~*I de-centre him, so he trips, falls and spills*~~
~~*a steady slaver of cadenced canto, seasoned*~~
~~*with risqué word play into my abyss of need*~~
~~*radiating a frenzy of fiery feelings*~~

~~*Too good to resist, how can I not*~~
~~*risk it all and tee-hee-hee!*~~
~~*Titter to the abattoir*~~
~~*frisking to face my fatality*~~
~~*for I am falling, deep into a gulch*~~
~~*where love bombs strike*~~
~~*and no one survives*~~

FALLING

*Love shots pump euphoria hormones into my aorta, inducing marbling to my
tenderloin, like a wagyu cow massaged throughout its life by a geisha boy & tickled
to its death by the tail feather of an albatross, only to end up a tomahawk steak
devoured
at full   T*

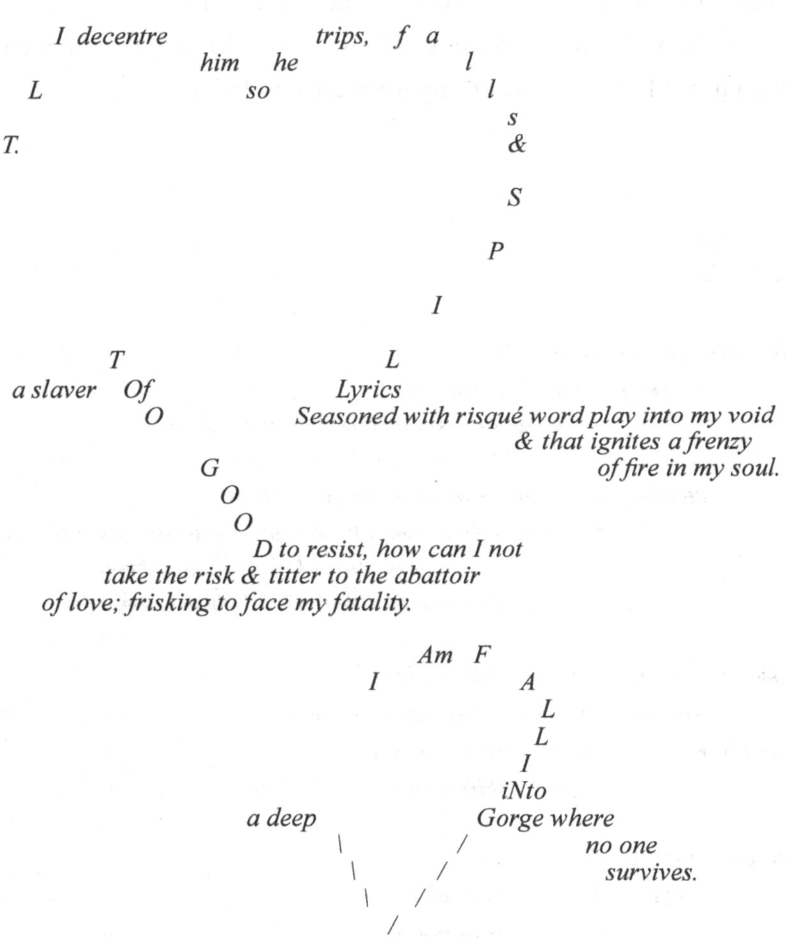

When I get no immediate response from Adam, I call him later that day to ask
him what he thought about my poem.

There is always a lot of background noise when we speak. Children
screaming, women shouting, but I'm not comfortable asking where the noise
is coming from. I resolve it's a typical ghetto racket and will not humiliate
Adam by bringing it up.

"*Wadii* this time?" Adam greets me in ghetto slang. "It's got a cute shape."

"Is that all you think? It took me days. No, weeks, to make it this concrete."

"I've got bigger problems than this Zoro. I'm feeling down right now, and really have lost the will to live."

My heart cracks because I can relate to cogitating over death.

"I used to have similar thoughts, but I go to therapy and that helps me find purpose in life. That's why I write my poems. I hope to publish a full collection one day."

He releases a prolonged, disparaging laugh. "Those are rich people's solutions. Us ghetto people don't do therapy…"

"I could help you…maybe get you a therapist from here? The one I use does online sessions…"

"Listen carefully to that word Zoro. THERAPIST. The Rapist!"

"What do you mean, the rapist? Tim would never!"

"Those fuckers rape your mind Zoro! They'll feed your head with all sorts of nonsense. I will never go to a therapist, even if I had the money to see one. I'd rather die… Hang on a minute. You said Tim? Why are you seeing a male therapist, Zoro? Is he white? Tim doesn't sound like a black name. Oh my God Zorodzai, you need to stop this nonsense!"

"He's in his sixties and he's harmless. I need someone to talk to, Adam. Someone mature and objective to help me make sense of life. Someone who won't say *but it's our culture* as his answer to all my life's problems."

"So you think some middle-aged white man will do that for you? You think he's going to understand your African problems?"

"He has offered me immense help to date, I've even managed to cut off toxic people and set boundaries that protec–"

"*Eish!* And look how lonely you are! Avoidance is not how we deal with African problems. How much do you pay this guy?"

"Sixty pounds per week…"

"Oh my God, Zorodzai! Wait, let me check the exchange rate right now and see…that's over a thousand Rand a week! Are you nuts?"

"Well maybe… that's why I'm seeing a therapist." I manage a weak laugh.

"No no no, this is crazy. How long have you been seeing this guy?"

"Two years…maybe three. I haven't really been counting the days. He is regulated and audited every year, he wouldn't do anything stupid… My meetings with Tim have been the one thing that's kept me sane over the years."

"Well, you have me now. You can tell your white Tim to fuck off!" We laugh together, but I can tell he means it. "Anyway, what's Wagyu? And what's a tomahawk?"

Yes, the poem!

"Wagyu is a breed of Japanese cattle valued for its marbled meat. A tomahawk is an expensive ribeye steak."

Adam goes quiet for a moment, and I suppose he is Googling. "Interesting," he finally says. "So why are you, an African woman, writing poems about expensive food, for me, a hungry African man?"

Immensely ashamed of my miscalculation, I change the topic.

I find myself buying gifts for Adam, lying to James that the single malt whiskies and expensive confectionery are for my friends. For the reunion. I send pictures of the offerings to Adam and ask him if he's ok with receiving gifts from me. I don't want to paint the wrong picture and only want to make up for the reality that we can't be together to exchange other acts of love.

He says he's very grateful for my thoughtfulness and that no woman has ever bought him gifts before. His words are encouraging. I want to give Adam something to look forward to, to make him feel better about life in general. I want to give him reasons to want to live, to show him I'm really preparing to be with him. And I want him to do the same, not necessarily in the form of gifts, but I need him to show me that he's excited, and that he'll be there. But Adam keeps his cool and says everything will work out.

HOW DO I TELL HIM?

That at the end of the day
when we stand face to face
with our tender meats swollen
with no clothes on—
all we have is each other
the space holding us together
the flow of rivers
the waves of oceans
and nothing else

Gormandising daily, I decide to focus on squats to firm up my expanding buttocks, and burpees to sculpt my supple abdomen. While I'm at it, I think to myself incessantly, *I need to be fit for our match. Wish I had the arse of an ass! I've been so inactive in bed; Will I let him down? What if my boobs sag suddenly? That porn I've been watching on my iPad is hot…I need to practise some of those moves so I can try them with Adam. Damn, I feel like I'm in my twenties again…*

I put on a pair of very short yellow cotton shorts I last wore the summer before I got pregnant with the twins, and a cream tank top with magenta polka dots. Feeling like a to-be-devoured raspberry ice-cream cone, I take a selfie of my backside and send it to Adam.

"*Maiwe! Zvaune dutu zve. Ndoda kuri paza!*" Adam exclaims that he loves the size of my rump, and although I see relatively mediocre buttocks in the mirror, I surrender to Adam's affirmation that fills me with happy endorphins.

"Are you not worried about my age Adam?" I ask him on a call one evening.

"*Ma small small awo.* Why do you ask?"

"Don't you think about having children?"

"Sometimes. But I'm not too bothered about that. My nieces and nephews are my children."

"I see."

"I've always dated older women."

"Why?"

"I'm not sure." He pauses, then continues, "Actually, I've never told this to anyone, but I was spiked and raped by an older woman when I was nineteen. A friend's mother. It was my first sexual encounter, and it totally messed me up for years. I've often thought the reason probably stems from that incident."

"Oh, I'm so sorry to hear that."

"But I also find women under the age of 35 extremely childish and materialistic. I just can't stand them."

"I think I might have a fear of abandonment, something that probably stems from being dumped in boarding school at a very young age. What I'm trying to say is, my heart is fragile, so please don't play with it. I've been through a lot, and I don't want to be taken for a ride, Adam." I can't believe how comfortable I am in my vulnerability when I open up to Adam.

"I love you with everything I have, Zoro."

"I love you too, Adam."

ONLY WORDS

I watch her suppressing a grin after decades of depression
and ask if she cares to share the joke. She squints and purrs:
'My pussy itches. Not because there's anything wrong with it.
It's been consistently wet for 81 days after 18 years of dryness.
Yeah, some men know how to resurrect the dead without even
touching them. Using words. Only words.

One day, after watching a documentary of how rampant HIV is in Southern Africa, I'm awoken to the risk I'm about to take. I send Adam a message, "We should test for HIV before I come there."

"No problem sweetness. I'll get the test done and share my results."

He doesn't. In the meantime, I Google how and where I can get tested locally, and I'm shocked to find I have to drive for an hour to the nearest Genitourinary Medicine Clinic. When I phone the clinic to make an appointment, I'm showered with uncomfortable personal questions and have to explain why I want the test, which is "only available to vulnerable people" or those who think they've been exposed to the virus. I tell them my husband is promiscuous, and I'm given an appointment, one week away. On the day I go to the GUM clinic, I wear joggers and an oversized hoodie to shield my identity, in case I bump into someone I know there. I ask to be tested for all STI's.

The test results take several days to come via text, and when they do, I screenshot and forward the messages to Adam who acknowledges receipt and says nothing further. I ask him again when he'll get his tests done, and he says, "Over here there are walk-in clinics where an HIV test is done on the spot, and the result comes out in minutes. We can even go together on the day you arrive."

"But I want to know your HIV status before I come all the way."

"Will you leave me if I test positive?"

I ponder the question and reply, "No."

"So, what's the point?"

"I don't want to expose James to the risk of HIV."

"Oh! I thought you said you don't sleep together anymore?"

"I didn't say that. I said we're no longer intimate. We barely have sex, but it does happen once in a while. I don't want to put his health at risk."

Four days before my flight to Zimbabwe, I receive a call from Royal United Hospital in Bath.

"Yes, I'm her mother." Terrified of what my daughter might have done to herself this time, the hairs on the back of my neck are already standing. *Oh God, I hope she's ok…alive!*

"Veem-baai was picked up unconscious from her campus room. She's in the ICU, currently stable, but has lost a lot of blood…"

Immediately, I know Vimbai has been slitting her wrists again. My world comes crashing down as the news sinks into my marrow. I get off the call and immediately ring James in Jersey where he's attending a conference. He says he'll catch the next flight back to England. I call St. Dubitrius and request that Peter boards for a few days. I pack a few essentials that I take to Peter before driving to Bath to station beside Vimbai. Like a lucid nightmare, everything is happening so fast, and although I seem to be in control, I feel derailed.

Upon arrival at the hospital, I find my daughter unconscious. I allow my tears to flow, wondering, *where the hell did I go wrong as a mother?* I rub her hand and plant a kiss on her forehead, whispering endless I love you's. After hours of feeling sorry for Vimbai and for myself, I realise it's impossible to leave the country, not now anyway. I call my boss the next morning to arrange extended carer's leave. I cancel my flight to Zimbabwe and flump back into the reality of being without Adam.

"Haurevesi!" When I break the news to Adam, his whisper of resignation stings.

"Ndorevesa." I feel his pain, as he feels mine.

A week later, Vimbai is discharged from hospital, and James and I take her home to Herefordshire where she requires round the clock care for a few weeks. Social workers and psychotherapists come in and out daily to assess and treat her.

I've plumped up several goose-feather scatter cushions and made her comfortable in the main lounge. I'm burning palo santo and white sage incense, constantly thinking of how else I can show my baby that she is loved and her life is worth living.

"What would you like to eat, my lovely?"

"I'm not hungry."

"Come on, you've got to try something. How about your favourite? Home-made guac with blue maize tortilla chips?"

"Go on then, mummy! And some devilled eggs!" It's lovely to see Vimbai's face light up to the prospect of food. She's recovering from anorexia.

I bring a few olive-green Ameraucana eggs to boil for six minutes while I gather ingredients for my special guacamole recipe – two creamy ripe avocados, half a red pepper because Vee won't have uncooked tomatoes, a small red onion, fresh key lime, dried chilli flakes and coriander leaf. After smashing the avo, chopping the onion and pepper, and squeezing out the lime juice, I mix it all together and sprinkle in the chilli and coriander. I sprinkle in some *fleur de sel* and leave the guac to stand in the fridge while I make the devilled eggs.

After placing the boiled eggs in cold water, I peel and halve them before scooping the yolks into a small bowl where I crush them. I sprinkle freshly chopped parsley and shallots, add dried paprika powder before mixing in low-fat mayonnaise and a pinch of Himalayan salt, until I reach a creamy consistency. Then I dust over some black pepper before scooping the mix into cool egg white halves. I open a fresh packet of blue tortilla chips then place the hors d'oeuvres on an oval bone china platter and...

"Daddy wants cheese and crackers as well mummy!"

"Coming right up!"

I sigh under my breath and grab some locally produced aged cheddar, French brie, goat's cheese and Italian cured meats from the fridge. Next to James's favourite assortment of cream crackers are black pitted olives, pistachios, figs and seedless green grapes that I neatly arrange on a small cheeseboard with cheese knives.

In between the bustle of looking after Vimbai and the boys, I make time to send Adam short, sweet poems.

This insatiable hunger for you
if only it were as easy to put out
as it is to put food to mouth
when the hollow of my gut calls

"I want to smell you Zoro," Adam says to me one day. "Send me your underwear, or nightdress. I want it unwashed. Something I can wear to sleep, so I can breathe you in and feel close to you."

Too self-conscious to send my large, unwashed underwear to South Africa, I choose an unwashed tank top instead. I open my bottom bedside drawer to retrieve the confectionary I've been collecting and hiding from Peter's feral appetite and James's inquisitive eyes. I find it all intact next to my pleasure toys, buried beneath my vibrant silk scarves printed with paisleys, florals, and chevrons. I box up the gifts and courier them, together with the tank top, to Adam's address in Yeoville.

Only a few days later, the blow of my cancelled plan comes with shocking revelations. Adam asks me to call him urgently, and when I do, he slurs gracelessly into the phone, telling me he had put his drinking on hold only because I had given him a reason to be happy again. Now, he has no choice but to return to the bottle to suppress his depression.

"We'll be ok my love. We'll come up with another plan."

"No. No. No, Zoro. It's all well and good for you to say that. You're there with your husband and children, trying to solve rich people's problems. You have something to fall back on. I have nothing! No wife, no children, no home. I have problems your sort could never imagine." I can't believe what Adam is saying. How he is saying it. As I try to adjust to his strange behaviour, Adam tumbles further into awkward territory. "Maybe it's just as well the trip is cancelled, Zoro. I didn't think it was a good idea for me to fuck another man's wife, anyway."

Something about the way he says this makes me feel dirty. And angry. "What did you say?"

"I've changed my mind!" *Oh God, no! Don't do this to me!* "I want you for myself Zoro. I want you to start divorce proceedings with your husband straightaway, if you really love me. Then you move here to live with me, or I come there to live with you."

"But you said you were comfortable dating a married woman, Adam. What's changed?"

"I love you Zorodzai. *Pane varume vose pasi pano, hakuna anokuda seni mudiwa wangu. Zvose pasi nokudenga, hakuna wandoda kudarika iwe. Aiwa hakuna!* My feelings for you are deeper than you'll ever know, and I'm no longer prepared to share you. Our culture doesn't take these things lightly. You know, being with another man's wife is taboo." While I'm flattered by Adam's words, I suddenly feel rushed off my feet and filled with doubt. *This was not part of our original plan!*

"I can leave James after we've met Adam. I need to see you first. For all I know, you don't exist."

"Zoro, do you think I'd ask you to take such a radical step if I wasn't serious about you? I'd never sell you dreams my darling. *Ndoda kuti uve wangu iwe.*"

"Well, I'm not sure I'd want to get married again, if I leave James."

"Why not? *Unoda kungoita zvechihure chete?*" Adam's insinuation that I'm simply whoring if I don't commit to him leaves me dumbstruck.

"Can't you see I'm dealing with a crisis right now?"

"Crisis!" Adam breaks into hysterics of condescending laughter. "Zorodzai, where have you ever heard of a Zimbabwean child slitting their wrists? That is white people's behaviour. You have a drama queen on your hands, my love. Someone who wants to kill themselves will just do it, ok. *Muendesei kumusha uyo, anodzoka ava bho!*" When he suggests Vimbai be sent to Zimbabwe to be straightened, I hang up on Adam and decide I'll never speak to him again.

The next morning, having slept fitfully, I'm reluctant to face the day. It is not my phone alarm that returns me to this realm of life. My other senses, attuned to the shift in energy in the room, have already alerted me to a dubious presence. I'm already on high alert when I at last force my eyelids open to find James hovering over me with my phone in his palm, pointing it at my face. I blink and it unlocks, then he turns it to his view and starts browsing. Consumed with sleep and shock, my reaction is delayed.

"James! What are you doing?"

"I didn't want to wake you up. The university fees invoice was emailed to you weeks ago and John's just told me it's overdue." James walks out of the bedroom with my mobile phone, his explanation blurring with each step towards our office, downstairs.

Good lord! I scramble out of bed and sprint down the hallway after James. Halfway down the stairs, I hear, "Get out of my room you little shit, I'm trying to have a private conversation here!" as Vimbai screams at Peter with utter contempt.

"Stop stealing my charger, you bum-sweat!" Peter's voice rings back with righteous indignation.

"I didn't steal it, I borrowed it!"

"Whatever!"

"Keep it down you two, I've got an assignment to hand in this morning." John cuts in.

"Out!" Vimbai demands. The familiar racket of bickering siblings reminds me that the kids are home, and I'm naked! Flying back upstairs to get dressed, I knock my left knee on the iron staircase balustrade and fall flat on my belly. I pick myself up from the thickly carpeted landing and enter our bedroom where I whisk my dressing gown. I put it on clumsily, desperately, as I rush back downstairs after James. By the time I get to him, he has found the email and has the invoice open, his online banking up on his PC screen. I stand next to him trying to control my panting, a whisper of apprehension lingering, and I await the consequences.

"Are you ok, Zoro? Here you go." James calmly hands back my phone, his eyes worried that I look worried. I snatch it out of his palm and quickly inspect my device history for his browsing trail. He doesn't seem to have seen anything. *Besides, this man is barely interested in anything I do. Why am I worried?*

I find messages of undying love from a sobered-up Adam, as if nothing happened the previous day. They're all unread. *Phew!* Adam doesn't seem to remember any of the offensive things he said last night, and that I hung up on him. When I confront him about his behaviour, Adam asks me to remind him what he said. I feel defeated and tell him to never mind.

"Eish, it's the ghetto in me, my sister. I'm a fuck up." is what Adam offers by way of apology, and I'm taken aback, not just by the self-deprecating words, but being called "my sister" by someone I'm having an affair with.

I decide to practise some guided yin yoga with a YouTube video to release the tension knotted in my muscles, and when I'm done, a surge of endocannabinoids floods my system until I feel intoxicated. Finding ways of getting high without consuming any substances is my preoccupation, and the main reason I've managed to stay off alcohol for so long.

Later that day, Adam acknowledges receipt and thanks me profusely for his parcel. He sends me a selfie of himself in my tank top, which makes me burst into titters.

Thinking about this morning's encounter with James, I set up double authentication on all my devices. I change passwords on all my social media apps and set a reminder to refresh the passwords weekly. *Just in case!* I can't help wondering if this was the first time James helped himself to my phone. *I think I'd know if he'd seen my interactions with Adam, though. Because no man in their right mind would keep calm after seeing such exchanges between their wife and another man.*

Several weeks later, when Vimbai is better, we all agree she should commute from home to university, and I volunteer to take her, a one and a half hour drive each way. I don't mind the drive, because I get to speak with Adam through my EarPods whilst driving. Vimbai has her headphones on, respecting my personal business.

I open up to Adam that I used to be dependent on alcohol, but I've been clean for two years now. He responds, *"Ah, waidombovavo drangad,"* and the quaintness of his Karanga accent makes me smile.

"Tim actually helped me quit alcohol. You too can stop if you want to, my love. All you need is the willpower to do it." I don't mention Michelle, my reiki practitioner. After the way Adam reacted to therapy, I can't divulge more about my self-care routines.

"So, what replaced the alcohol?"

"Tea, believe it or not! I've fallen in love with herbal tea – turmeric for breakfast, ginger for elevenses, rooibos for high tea, chamomile before bed. I've been known to experiment with other herbals when I'm not flirting with Earl Grey in between meals. I'm now a self-proclaimed connoisseur of global infusions. And one day, I'll tell you all about how I like my tea made, in the different teapots I've collected from all over the world," I laugh at my own forbearance.

"Different teapots? *Eh…*"

"Yup, my favourite being the Japanese Tetsubin, followed by Ethiopian Jebena."

"Do you own a Kango from home?"

"Of course! I love my brown Kango teapot as well, but it's quite big and I tend to use it when we have Zimbabwean guests visiting."

As the days progress, Adam and I begin to talk about things besides looking forward to having hot wild sex. We enjoy discovering any little parallels in our vastly distinctive universes. Like how we both lost our mothers to breast cancer, or how our annoyingly demanding fathers both learnt at Mukaro Mission – they battered our mothers, those men, and we find it painful to talk about. How Adam has an aged diviner uncle based in Ngundu and I also have a late great aunt who lived in Chivi, who was a spirit medium.

We believe our lineages are the reason we are spiritually pegged, and we cling onto this belief like flies to faeces.

We both love music, art and literature. Our taste in Zimbabwean music is also very similar, except for Zimdancehall which I think is a form of poetry, and Adam thinks is utter nonsense "because it lacks consciousness". And I cite the likes of Winky D and Tocky Vibes, arguing that they and many more are philosophical in their music. He loves Jamaican reggae music though, and I learn a lot about it from him. Before I know it, I've got a selection of Jah Rastafarians on my playlist – from the vintage classic Bob Marley to the modern classic Jah 9, and often find myself Googling the lyrics in their music and learning about the history of Lij Tafari Maikonnen, Emperor of Ethiopia later known as Haile Selassie I.

Adam goes on to create a private music playlist with 45 videos for me on YouTube, which I watch or listen to when I can't speak with him. Some of my favourite tracks on it include Pink Floyd's *Wish you were here*, Tracy Chapman's *All you have is your soul*, and The Head and the Heart's *Rivers and roads*. I find it hilarious that he has also included Andy Brown's *Many cows* on the list.

A few days later, Adam creates a slideshow of his favourite photos of me, with Emeli Sande's *Lifetime* as the theme song. I'm amazed by Adam's generosity in his display of love, I sometimes wonder if it's sustainable.

Sometimes he texts me links to the music he's listening to at 3 am. I'm occasionally surprised by his music choices, mostly because I've not listened to the songs in a while – *Chamakuwende*, by Stella Chiweshe, *Chitima Nditakure* by Thomas Mapfumo, *Kumatendera* by Mbira dzeNharira, *Nhemamusasa* by Chiwoniso Maraire, and other music I would not necessarily seek out. We discuss vintage and contemporary Zimbabwean music in depth, citing how the history and culture of our country is hidden in these beautiful gems.

Occasionally Adam gives me random football updates. "It was the Champions League today. Real Madrid vs Chelsea. Went to extra time."

I'm not interested in football but respond enthusiastically, "Wow!" I know his team is Arsenal and I ask him whether they're winning whenever he mentions they're playing.

Everything about my mundane life seems to interest Adam and it feels like we're on each other's minds every breathing moment.

I tell Adam I no longer practise Christianity, ever since I learnt it was the white man's weapon of choice to drive slavery and colonisation; I'm now into New Age spirituality and I believe in the power of nature to heal. I share that I wear crystal gems as they give me positive energy.

"They balance your chakras," I explain.

"Oh, so you're one of those 'chakra huns'? What are they anyway, these chakras?"

"They're energy points in your body. Let me send you links so you can read up on it."

"You're too westernised *mwana wevhu*! Does that stuff really work?"

"Of course it works! A simple way of looking at it is, don't do too little or too much of anything, and you'll be ok. Anyway, most of my spiritual practice is based on Eastern, not Western teachings. And you'll be surprised by how similar the Eastern beliefs are with African spirituality. Besides, nature is universal. Stones are stones and they're all Mwari's creations, whether they're in Europe, America, Asia or Africa. The world-renowned Shona sculptures – are they not made of quartz, serpentine, verdite, jasper, dolomite, stromatolite, opal, jade, lepidolite, you name it? All those stones are semi-precious gemstones with healing and protective energies. It is said, the stone calls the artist and dictates how it will be sculpted. Zimbabwe is rich, my love. When you place a Shona sculpture in your home, it's more than just for decoration."

"That's interesting!"

"Us humans are intimately connected with crystals, and even our blood is a form of liquid crystal. I've invested a lot of time investigating how to heal and be happy, so my daily rituals focus on the manufacturing of positive energy and my spiritual wellbeing."

"*Zvema* rituals *hazvisi zvekuroya here izvo?*" He chuckles as he asks me whether I practice witchery and I laugh.

"No, my love. It's as simple as using essential oils and salts to bath, burning incense, and things like that to cleanse my aura. *Hanti chero ku*church they burn incense? It's to get rid of negative energy. I also meditate daily. Those are all rituals."

One day, I receive a call from my uncle, Gweje, who teaches humanities at the University of Zimbabwe. I've been dying to tell someone about Adam, but I can't, at least not directly. I use the opportunity to ask him something that has been on my mind, "*Nhai* Sekuru Gweje, why is it ok in our culture, for married men to cheat, but not the women?"

"Who told you that our culture doesn't allow women to cheat? That's an Elizabethan notion, *muzukuru*. Have you forgotten the Shona proverb, *Gombarume harina mwana*? Before the whites brought their Christianity and their ways, it was a well-known and accepted practice, that a married woman could have a lover to placate her desires, as long as they didn't make it obvious or disrespect the husband. The husband would go drinking in nearby villages till late, knowing fully that he was allowing his wife space, and on his return into his homestead, he'd deliberately sing loudly as he approached, to give the lover an opportunity to escape. If the lover was careless enough to impregnate the married woman, the child would belong to her husband. That's where the proverb comes from. And this practice is still very much alive in some rural parts of Zimbabwe."

On hearing this, I internally ululate for my redemption. Sekuru Gweje's explanation further cements my belief that marriage is a manmade concept that sets up humankind for failure - a social experiment that went wrong, and too far gone for anyone to admit it. People who truly love each other should not have to compromise so much in exchange for loyalty, as they will eventually lose their sense of self and become resentful. And at that point it will become some sort of contest on who can make the other more miserable until death separates them. I believe my relationship with James might have turned out better if we'd stayed unmarried. I'm certain, if I divorce James, I'll never marry again.

I BELONG TO NOBODY

(After Lesley Gore's 'You don't own me')

*I belong to **nobody***

*Belong I **nobody** to*

*To I **nobody** belong*

***Nobody** to belong I*

A few weeks later, I have a long call with my older sister Sharai, who lives with her family in America. She tells me about her favourite actors, Kerry Washington and Tony Goldwyn, who she says are both married but worked together in a TV series called *Scandal*.

"They are definitely twin flames," she says. I begin to research "twin flames" and realise that is exactly what me and Adam are. When I share some links with Adam, he too buys into it. Every single article avows our relationship is a spiritual union, ticking all the boxes of *20 signs that you have met your twin flame*.

This becomes the driving force behind our ecstatic union. Adam is my "twin flame" with whom I have an unexplainable knowing, and James is my "soulmate", with whom I've battled to love, my logical mind thinking I should stay as our relationship looks great on paper, but my intuition telling me to leave. Both men will teach me specific life lessons that will lead me to a "life partner". I cannot imagine anything beyond Adam.

THINGS SAID IN A LANGUAGE WE DON'T DREAM IN

Why do we say things we don't mean?
Things said in a language we don't dream in,
undertaking to abide by rules we don't grasp;
solemn vows made up by Thomas Cranmer,
oaths that even non-believers agree to
recite in the house of the Lord.

Robed in attires with names we can't pronounce,
we slaughter beasts bigger than our budgets and spread
buffets wider than our guest lists: our mothers, fathers,
their siblings with their own guest lists: small houses, exes
and their own lists of guests clueless why they're there;
to make promises in their presence, of things we can't do.

Adam and I talk about our favourite books. I like to read literature by African women authors, like Francesca Ekwuyasi's _Butter Honey Pig Bread_, Jennifer Nansubuga Makumbi's _The First Woman_, Sue Nyathi's _A Family Affair_, Cynthia Rumbidzai Marangwanda's _Shards_, and many others.

He says, "You want to change the world order? _Siyana nezve feminism izvo!_" and recommends that I read _The Alchemist_ by Paulo Coelho, _Echoing Silences_ by Alexander Kanengoni, _Mayombe_ by Pepetela, _The Healers_ by Ayi Kwei Armah and _Revelations_ by Mongane Wally Serote. He also recommends the Bible as one of the best anthology of stories to have ever been published. "I've read it a few times for entertainment, my darling. Not for the doctrine." He chuckles at his own triviality.

I'm a bit thrown off by Adam's comment about feminism so I say to him, "How can I quit feminism when I was raised in a stifling society that doesn't see beyond my sex? Do you even understand what feminism is?"

"We can't be equal, _wangu._"

I had a feeling he had exaggerated his respect and compassion for women in the beginning, just to win my heart. But I know he'll come around and be proper as our relationship develops, so I decide to not challenge him further. I buy all the books he recommends, send him pictures of myself holding them, but never read them.

I love gardening, and absolutely adore my plants. When it's springtime, I share my cornucopia of sprouting perennials with Adam, and at first, he feigns interest in pictures of my flowers, but one day I tell him about my geraniums and how they remind me of back home, and he asks, "*Anodhliwa here maruva awo?*" His lack of interest in my plants slowly poisons my passion for them, and I begin to neglect my treasured garden.

Sometimes I'm aware of how much my character conflicts with Adam's, but I choose to ignore it. After all, *opposites attract and all that*. Plus, we might never meet. When I think about that, I beat myself up for jinxing that part of our relationship. But it doesn't stop me from falling deeper. And deeper.

He wants to see pictures of everything I eat and drink, so each morning, I send him shots of my bowl of granola, served with fresh berries and Greek yoghurt, soused with organic Canadian maple syrup. Or, grilled halloumi, with cherry tomatoes sautéed in truffle oil, and avocado slices on buttered gluten-free granary toast.

"Gluten-free *zvomboreveiko?*" he asks me on a call.

"Gluten is a protein naturally found in certain grains, like wheat, so I can't eat anything made from wheat. I buy wheat-free or gluten-free food so that I don't get sick."

"What happens when you eat gluten?"

"I get bloated…"

"Ha! Zoro…you mean to say farting is a problem?" He laughs hysterically while I roll my eyes with mild annoyance.

"Yes, when you fart, your body is trying to communicate that it doesn't like what you fed it. I might get inflammation as well."

"And what's that?"

"Inflammation is the body's immune response. You know if you're injured, you'll get a swelling – that's the body's way of saying, 'I'm hurting, don't touch!'. The body does the same thing when you feed it things it's allergic or intolerant to. Have you ever woken up with a stiff, sore neck, as if you positioned your neck wrong while you were sleeping? That's inflammation. Or unexplained throbs or swelling in your joints, especially the ankles...?"

"Yeah, I get that a lot when I've had a lot to drink. How did you find out about what you're intolerant to?'

"I went to see a nutritionist. I'd been feeling unwell and after running every test there is, my GP couldn't figure out what was wrong with me. That's when I decided to take a holistic approach to my wellbeing, and since I began following my prescribed diet, I feel brand new."

"*Eh!* You have money to burn. Some of us just eat everything. After all, we must not discriminate against the things Mwari made available for us to eat."

"Well, you have the privilege of daily sunshine in Africa. Your body can deal with most things you expose it to when your body has an abundance of vitamin D. Most of my digestive issues are triggered by the lack of sun over here. Vitamin D deficiency has insurmountable ripple effects, from depletion of digestive enzymes to dysbiosis of the gut microbiome. And then depression! Literally nothing works without it..."

"I see. *Ko* holistic *zvorevei?*"

"It's a multicultural, multi-disciplinary way of living your life, and it encompasses emotional, social, physical and mental health. For example, I choose to never take chemicals and modern medicines for ailments I can heal naturally. You could say love is the core of holistic healing."

"Love?"

"Yes. Self-love. And love for Mwari's creations."

A few days later, I'm cooking for James and the kids whilst chatting online with Adam. The spicy, citrusy fragrance of my stir-fry is as intoxicating as the love in the air. I grind in some Celtic salt then send Adam pictures of the golden lemon-infused tiger prawns sizzling in chilli olive oil on a large cast iron skillet, with freshly chopped garlic and dried basil flakes sprinkled over them, and he can't believe "those creatures are safe for human consumption?" I chuckle at Adam's self-contradictory remarks.

Ever so proud of growing my own, I carefully harvest fresh herbs and vegetables from large wooden troughs in the south-facing corner of my garden to make red potato and green pea pasta bakes, and when I share my pictures and step-by-step process videos with Adam, he's fascinated by my lifestyle, especially that people still cook in ovens. In South Africa, he could never dream of such a luxury due to the frequent load shedding. "We only have one hour to cook when the electricity comes back. Sometimes, that happens at 10pm, after a whole day with nothing. It's also pointless to have fridges *sha*. It's so hot and with intermittent electricity, food just rots."

"You should consider growing your own vegetables, maybe keep a few chickens. That way, you cook fresh when you have electricity. Also, homegrown food is soul food."

"How so?"

"When you are intentional, plants respond to the love and energy you expend whilst nurturing them, and that energy will in turn benefit you when you consume them. I believe they taste a lot better too. Plus you'll derive happiness from the time you spend connected with the earth whilst tending to them."

"And the chickens?"

"Same concept. You look after them with love, ensuring they're raised in conditions conducive to their overall wellbeing. And you choose to kill them humanely so that their flesh nourishes your body as opposed to poisoning it."

"Ha, you will never not intrigue me, *mudiwa wangu*." It melts my heart when he refers to me as *his love* in chiShona. I can spend hours on end imagining him saying those words to my face, gently whispering them in my ear, and the warm, wet kisses accompanying them.

When I send him pictures of my wild mushroom risotto neatly garnished with a twig of fresh parsley, and a bundle of succulent herb-roasted asparagus on the side, he asks whether we have guests coming, and says he wishes he was eating with me. My heart sinks.

"Those vegetable stalks look weird. What do they taste like?"

"Asparagus? It's got a nutty, buttery sweetness with a slight jot of bitterness. Its flavour hugely depends on how you cook it or what you pair it with. It can sometimes have an earthy, grassy taste that I absolutely adore!"

"*Ko* where's the meat?" he asks, and I tell him I'm detoxing because it's unhealthy to consume meat daily, especially red meat, like we did back home in Zimbabwe. "*Huye bodo!*" he remarks with a laughing emoji.

When I ask him what he's eating, he mentions things like bread and boiled eggs for dinner, and I feel ashamed for eating better than he does, for the luxury of affording food he would never dream of eating. It makes me want to take him under my wings, to look after him, to elevate him until he is sophisticated, like James.

Sometimes he sends me pictures of *bhodho*, where he goes with friends to buy *sadza nenyama* cooked in cast iron cauldrons on the streets of Johannesburg. How I miss the fire-cooked *mugaiwa* with unbleached, wood-smoked offal that he has access to. He doesn't believe me when I say I envy some of his meals.

One evening, he calls me excitedly to say he bought a tin of pilchards at the local grocery store and wants to know what fancy dish he can make with that? While I'm not a huge fan of his choice of fish, I'm delighted to talk him through making a quick fried-rice bowl. He only needs to stir-fry diced shallots and red peppers in shallow vegetable oil, then add stock-boiled rice, beaten egg, seasoned with table salt and white pepper. Once the fried rice is served in a bowl, he can top it with warmed pilchards and freshly chopped cherry tomatoes. He sends me a picture of his meal, proactively garnished with 3 wilting cucumber slices. There's a pint of lager on the side and the picture is captioned, "I want to marry you!" to which I respond with clapping, laughing, crimson heart, and fire emojis – two of each.

I look forward to gossiping with Adam about other Zimbabweans on social media. He has shown me most of his family, sending me links to their social media profiles and narrating their backstories until I know their birthdays, wedding anniversaries, and where they work. I even know when they're "not watching TV these days" because they're waiting for Adam to pay for their DSTV subscription in South Africa when he gets paid.

When there's a death in his family, Adam travels to Zimbabwe and I send him $350 *chema* to help with the associated costs. Adam is shocked by this act of generosity, but I'm so out of touch with translating the value of money, I say I understand the challenge of feeding funeral guests, but really, I had no idea it was "too much money".

I try to downplay my success and life of luxury but fail miserably.

On a video call, Adam notices the paintings on our walls and the furniture in our house, and he asks where I bought the items, and how much they cost.

An impasto painting hung above me vibrantly depicts an English countryside landscape. Multi-coloured daubs of acrylic paint have been thrown, splattered and flicked onto canvas in many layers to create a shower of wildflowers, elevated from the surface to give texture pleasing to see and touch. When I tell him that single painting cost £8,000, he winces.

"It reminds me of my own springtime garden, so I tend to appreciate this piece more during the winter months when the garden is in hibernation." He seems to ponder my offering but says nothing. "It took us years to pay for it," I lie, then change the subject when I realise he's not succumbing to my tale.

"Tell me what it's really like over there. The xenophobia we hear about on TV. I worry about you so much when I hear that another Zimbabwean has been killed in South Africa. Just the other day I came across a Twitter account dedicated to propagating the hatred of foreigners in South Africa. How crazy is that!"

"It's bad Zoro, but what can I do? Can you imagine being bathed in gasoline and ignited alive? *Hai*…where is the African unity in that?" He pauses for a moment to swallow the pain in his voice then says, "What's racism like over there?"

"It can be bad, especially in poor areas, but with all the noise about Black Lives Matter, it's more subtle now. Besides that, one advantage of the UK over other countries is that, if you work hard and manage to move into a good neighbourhood, the racism is a lot less malignant there."

"What, you're saying rich whites are not racist?"

"No. I'm saying the educated and well-travelled whites are better at hiding it. For example, instead of attacking you for being black, they might simply move out of a neighbourhood they feel is becoming contaminated by blacks." He briefly releases a suppressed laugh, and I carry on, "Also, it's not all of them who are racist. It's a systemic issue, just like not all men are misogynists."

He says "*Eish*!" and changes the topic.

I'm enamoured by Adam because he has the guts to say what he really thinks, whether it hurts me or not. That, to me, is authentic love. No one has ever been so free with me. I too feel free to say the craziest things I'd never dare say to James, or any other person. I want to experience this for the rest of my life, but for now, all we have is now.

MISS YOU

> *night sky*
> *diamond encrusted—*
> *i see you*

I've been buying new clothes and wearing a bit of make-up, even though Adam says he doesn't care much for it. I've been getting my hair done every week too, because I want to send Adam beautiful pictures, and compete with any younger, fatter women that might float into his horizon while he waits for us to meet.

For the first time in years I look in the mirror and see myself. I do not wonder where James's dark shadow has disappeared to because I glow better without it.

My youthful elegance and self-esteem are becoming pronounced, and this seems to interest James. He looks at me funny these days, as if he's stunned that a woman my age could feel energised and eager to live again. He suddenly wants to spend more time with me, taking me out to expensive restaurants and to be seen with me in public.

"Come with me to play golf, baby."

"You know I'm not interested in golf, James." What I mean is *I'm not interested in you, James.*

"Just tag along as my caddie. Let's enjoy some quality time in the sun together." He corners me for a kiss, and I compress my lips to avoid betraying Adam. It feels awkward to be wanted by James again, especially now that I've moved on emotionally and have a younger boyfriend to die for.

"Fine, I'll come with you."

One afternoon, Adam asks me to call him. It sounds urgent, so I find a quiet space in the garden and phone him immediately. In monotone speech, Adam shares that he is in a dark place and needs help.

"Oh my love, I feel helpless. How about you do something that might boost your morale. Maybe go outside and take a walk. A long walk, not the 5-minute walk to the garage to buy alcohol. Or go to the mall and treat yourself to a plant. Maybe a bright poster or painting to brighten up your house. Maybe even a scented candle to uplift your mood. It would be good for you to take a break from drinking. Did you read that article I sent you on how to meditate…"

"We don't do that here! *Ini* I'm ghetto *zve*."

"Adam, you need to give it a try. I promise you, it works…"

"You're not listening to me!" he bellows back. "You never listen to me! I don't want to go anywhere or do anything. I especially don't want to buy anything!"

"I can understand that…"

"No, you don't! You don't understand me at all."

"What I understand is that you're going through a lot and I'm trying to offer you practical solutions to whatever it is… Listen, there are things that are known to make anyone going through stuff feel better. This is why I'm making these suggestions. What else can I do to help you in my absence…"

"When I talk to you Zoro, I feel like I've gone out for a walk in the park, or the forest. I feel so energised, and all my problems just disappear in those moments. And that's exactly what I need right now. I want to talk to you. I want to say all the things I need to say, and I need you to listen." I can't understand why anyone would want to vent without expecting practical solutions to their problems. *What is the point, unless you actually enjoy being stuck in that sullen state!*

I immediately remember how Tim explained "energy vampires" to me when we were discussing people with narcissistic tendencies. I realise how weary I feel after speaking to Adam when he's going through his episodes. It's beginning to bother me that Adam never appears to seek solutions to his problems but prefers to wallow in them and expects me to whine with him, or cheer his droning, encouraging him to drink through his woes.

That evening, the first tweet I see when I open the Twitter app says, "No amount of love can fix someone if they enjoy being broken."

I feel drained and begin drafting a message to end things with Adam.

There's no easy way to say this, but I think we should end our affair. I don't think I'm any good for you. I don't know how to conduct myself in this relationship. Perhaps it's because I haven't quite healed from my past. I keep hurting you and perhaps I also expect too much from you. It's not sustainable. I feel like I should return to myself, in prayer and meditation, and stop expecting anything from anyone. While I will not be happier doing that, I know I won't be as nervous, agitated, impatient, worried, afraid – all these negative feelings that seem attached to our love. Love and fear can't coexist. Thank you for seeing me, loving me, empowering me. I will forever be grateful for the love you've shown me. I'm sorry...

I can't bring myself to send it. Instead, I find myself reaching into James's wine chiller for some Pinot Grigio. I hold the bottle for a good few minutes, pondering what I'm about to do. *Perhaps I could do just a bit of yoga and I'll be fine. Remember, if you can control breath, you can control the mind and life force, if you can control the mind, you can control life force and breath, and if you can control life force, you can control breath and mind. I haven't meditated in a while… But one small glass won't hurt either.*

After two long years, the rim of a wine glass finally kisses my lips, and *Jesus Christ of Nazareth! This is far more beautiful than a Zambezi sunset.* I savour the elegant aromas of apricots and almonds as the cool, dry, citrusy fluid flows down my wanting gullet. It goes straight to my head and down below, and as I take another swig, I marvel at wine's underhanded ability to be in more than one place at the same time. *Oh how I've missed this gorgeous nectar of joy!*

Later that night, when my temper has eased, I play with Judah then send Adam a message on WhatsApp. I share with him an online link to twenty ways he can acquire positive energy. The first "way" says, "Houseplants are the perfect partners for your self-care routine. Take a moment to tend to them, and they'll nourish your soul in return." I'm able to articulate that the solutions I was suggesting earlier were meant to be positive sources of energy for him, far better than trying to sap ready-made energy from other people.

He responds, "*ndezvekumama izvo!*" and goes AWOL. I try to meditate, but I can barely calm my mind for ten minutes, whereas I could previously sit for hours on end in quiet contemplation, practising detachment from the senses. A short session of yoga now feels like a triathlon, so I tend to talk myself out of it. When Adam's playing up, playing with Judah feels like a chore. It seems so much easier to drink more wine.

While my love is AWOL, I do house chores to the music of Leonard Dembo, intoning and occasionally swaying to *Nzungu Ndamenya:*

> *...nzembe yangu yatorwa naaaniko?*
> *Ndatsvaka mudendere mayo ndaishayaaaaaa!*

Adam resurfaces three days later and sends me links to two songs on YouTube without explaining why he had disappeared. The first is Pink Floyd's *Wish You Were Here.* He captions it, "my current most played song". The second is Tupac Shakur's original *Until The End of Time.* He captions it, "This song is on repeat every morning. It's the original song, not one of the two variations that was officially released. The hook makes me want to cry, and so does the sincerity of the lyrics. People don't understand art. Tupac wanted it this way for a reason."

We've always agreed that Tupac is the best poet of all time, and Adam knows I have a soft spot for the rapper. We've had many short-lived discussions over the West-Coast-East-Coast hip hop saga and both agree that the West Coast by far produced the best rap music in the 90s, contrary to the debates I've had with James, who's a die-hard fan of the East Coast. The mention of Tupac immediately awakens the teenager in me. The one that wore sagging jeans and bodysuits, now known as leotards, always with a bright-coloured, checked flannel shirt tied round my waist in the African heat. Large metal hoop earrings hanging on either side of my tanned baby face, paisley print bandana tightly wrapped around my generously gelled hair, with black "Bad Boys" combat leather boots by Bata to complete the look.

We're all soldiers in God's eyes, was one of my favourite lines from Tupac's *Me and my girlfriend,* and I had secretly crushed on the rappers on tv, fantasising about being one with them. There had been no social media or Google those days to research the American ghetto lifestyle, or to look up words such as "groupie" that I didn't quite understand, yet I badly wanted to be one anyway.

Those had been the best days of my teenage life. I felt like a Californian gangster whore, for writing dirty rap song lyrics in "auto-books" I swapped with my friends in high school – these were exercise books we should have used for notetaking but instead curated our favourite things in life in them, like music, films and our favourite celebrities, a bit like social media today. Doing all that whilst maintaining high academic grades and ensuring no one from Girls Church Union caught wind of my free-spiritedness had been the peak of my childhood devilment.

I and my friends wanted to go to America and to be American, oblivious to how the blacks in America equally wanted to be in Africa, and to be African – artificially inflating their breasts and buttocks with silicon and swelling their lips with Botox, tanning their skin and giving their children African names to connect with the continent.

My sister, who also wanted to be American, had eventually gone there and learned the truth, but when I heard it from her, I refused to assimilate, thinking instead that Sharai was gatekeeping. It was only later in life when I'd migrated to the UK that I stopped taking my roots for granted and began appreciating my Africanness in the context of the global village. And when I'd eventually visited Sharai in America and seen first-hand how the blacks in the ghettos lived, I thought myself lucky to have grown up in Zimbabwe.

When the rappers I loved began dying like flies from shooting one another, I'd been too young to understand the true impact of what was going on. The murders were never properly investigated. There was barely media coverage of activism for black lives at the time.

Despite all that, my childhood dream of becoming a gangster whore with a real nigga from the ghetto is awakening, like one's true life purpose. I love my wild imagination, and I'm grateful for my connection with Adam. I'm old enough to know that love isn't perfect—it can't be. All I want is a man who can heal my paralysed heart and make me feel again. Adam is not just a mender of my heart; he's a teacher of life who makes me feel alive and frees me from mental slavery. Whenever I dwell on his shortcomings, I recall these lines from The Forty Rules of Love by Elif Shafak:

While pretty flowers are instantly plucked, few people pay attention to plants with thorns and prickles. But the truth is, great medicines are often made from these.

Appreciating in that moment how beautiful the pang of longing is, I joyfully do the butterfly dance to Tupac's *Do for Love*, one of my favourite bangers that aptly paints the tumultuous nature of love amidst the convolution of human nature.

"I'm a very spiritual man," Adam says to me one day.

"But you can't even be bothered to meditate or self-care…"

"Those are Western ways of practising spirituality."

"Adam, a spirit is a spirit. We're not talking about religion here. Spirituality goes beyond skin colour, location and culture. It's about your soul's personal relationship with Mwari, despite where and how you were raised. How do you show Mwari that you love and appreciate Her? How do you practise your spirituality? Is the practice documented?"

"We honour our ancestors. That is Shona spirituality."

"And you think that's enough to cultivate your personal relationship with Mwari?"

"Shona spirituality is not a religion but sacred science. I get through to Mwari via the ancestors."

"But how do you do it? Talk me through the practice? What do you say to the ancestors? And what do the ancestors say back to you when they've spoken to Mwari on your behalf? Do you understand their language? Where is the Shona spirituality handbook on what needs to be done? How can I learn it…Ever heard of universal oneness?"

"Do you mean *ubuntu?*"

"Not quite, but it's similar. Universal oneness means we're one with Mwari and everything created by Her, meaning we are all interconnected through our creation by Mwari. We live within ecosystems and those ecosystems are very much a part of us. Think of all the bacteria in our bodies controlling everything we do, from our appetites to our life's desires, and so on. That's a proper rabbit hole I don't want to get into right now."

"Right…sounds like Rastafarian Livity."

I quickly Google *livity* and find it is the belief that all living things are connected to the divine. "Exactly! I may as well be Rastafarian! It also means, Mwari already knows your thoughts and feelings, so isn't it a bit pointless for you to communicate with Her through others when She already knows what you think and feel? Also, you are me and I am you. If I hurt you, I hurt myself, and vice versa. Every thought, action and event is connected to anything and everything else."

"Okay."

"You need to figure out why you feel so empty inside Adam. Cultivate your relationship with Mwari and other relationships that matter to you, then you will find purpose and not feel so devitalised. When we first 'met' we both shared this emptiness, but getting to know you has made me feel less empty. You make me happy, and you definitely have filled the void that used to consume me. Don't you feel better for having me in your life?" Adam does not respond.

"About your spirituality, well, from where I stand, your relationship with Mwari is clear. You hate yourself so much with all the things you do to self-sabotage. You're basically saying to Mwari 'You wasted your time creating me' and every time you deliberately self-hurt, you emphasise to Her that you hate yourself and you hate Her. Because you and Mwari are one."

"*Haaa*, let's leave this discussion for another day."

Having experienced several drunken encounters with Adam, it has become clearer to me that he has an unhealthy relationship with alcohol, worse than I had it, and I'm determined to make him see how bad the situation is by telling him how alcohol eroded my stomach lining and made me susceptible to some of my food intolerances.

I worry daily that alcohol will kill Adam, if the xenophobic South Africans don't kill him first.

When Adam finds a bit of money, he disappears for days on end, and gets drunk to the point of "feeling" death. He seems to like that he can "taste, see and smell death" as he puts it, when he shares some of his drunken experiences with me.

I can't stop him. Even if I try to speak with him during those days, it's pointless, because we can't understand each other. Except that we love each other, and I feel him more intensely in his absence. When he disappears on his multi-day benders, I join him in spirit, with one glass at first, then two, then the whole bottle, and James points out that I ought to be careful with my drinking. I turn to his arms when Adam's nowhere to be found, and I feel guilty for cheating on Adam.

Adam hates it when I do anything with James, so I've stopped talking about James with him. But Adam is highly intuitive and texts or tries to call precisely when James is removing my clothes. And when I try to explain why I didn't pick up immediately, he says, "Comrade, you're not going to leave James for me, are you?" Then he goes on a questioning rampage of why I'm cheating on my husband, again. When I try to explain my history of emotional abuse, and now the lack of a connection between me and James, that I love him instead, I stop midway and realise I can't even remember why I'm doing it.

I'm frustrated by how Adam and I fell in love without really thinking things through, and the situation is driving me insane. I remind Adam about James cheating on me in our early years of marriage, and he hoots, "You allowed it! And if you didn't leave him then, you'll never leave him now."

"Where I come from, cheating is not exactly a valid reason to leave a husband. All my aunts advised me to stay put, *gomera uripo*, when I sought their counsel. In the family I grew up in, cheating men are as unassailable as rain falling from the sky. It will happen, whether you like it or not."

"You're not a victim Zoro. You choose to be in a situation you claim is bad for you. You're an independent career woman, and even if you weren't, divorcing that man will earn you half of everything he's ever worked for. You'd never struggle on your own. Plus there's maintenance!" I'm jarred by

Adam's suggestions, and while I think of a response, he carries on, "You should have left him. At least he has changed now and seems like he's trying to do what is best for his family. He sounds like a great guy to me, actually. Because most people don't change." Adam's altered tune dupes me, and his new views make me feel like an ungrateful husband basher, like *I* am the villain. "And have you never done wrong in your marriage, my darling?" he adds.

"What? Not that I'm aware of…"

"Now now Zoro, that can't be entirely true."

"Well, I may have skipped cooking a meal when I didn't feel like it. Other than that, I really have done my best to be a good wife. And if you're wondering if I've ever cheated before, the answer is no. I'm sure it's pretty easy to tell by how difficult I've found it to conduct myself in this relationship. I haven't been with any other man in my life."

"Your husband is emasculated, shame!" I don't bother asking Adam to elaborate and decide I've had enough of this madness.

ISN'T IT AWFUL?

The shame

you feel

for something

someone

(else)

did to you

I tell Adam I can't do this anymore. We agree to part ways amicably. I spend the next few days sobbing into my pillow at night and writing haiku and other short poems to grieve for my lost love.

LOVE LOST

he's not with me

the spore beneath the fern's frond

has nowhere to fall

About a week later, Adam sends me a message and says he cannot do this; the loneliness is killing him. He sends me a link to Leonard Zhakata's *Hauchada Here* on YouTube. When I listen to the *Sungura* maestro lamenting an estranged wife in his classic quivering croon, I imagine my dear Adam on his knees, grovelling. All my faculties ebb, and we rekindle our love.

But something has changed. Adam now prefers to text and avoids my calls. When I confront him about his shift in attitude, he says we are prone to fight more during voice calls, so it's best to stick to messaging for now. Most times, Adam takes longer than usual to respond to my messages, and says he fell asleep unexpectedly after overeating *sadza*, or got too drunk and knocked out without texting me back, or that there was no electricity. When I ask him again why his communication has become intermittent, he accuses me of being insufferable.

"Why does it bother you when I challenge you, Adam?"

"It's how you say it, Zorodzai. How you phrase it! You can be immensely disrespectful!"

NO LONGER YOUR PEACE

You hold onto me like your first Jesus piece
telling me daily that nothing's changed

Yet it's clear as day that I'm no longer your peace
lying that you love me, yet you've walked out the door

Deserted in this situation-ship, I await stale crumbs
like I'm in a desert, starving and yearning for your love

I'm worn-out, running around on this hamster wheel
chasing after you, your time and your love

Vimbai has become more stable lately, so I resuscitate my plans to meet Adam to dissipate the growing tension.

"Shall we plan another trip, my love? Things are a little more stable here."

"Yes, that would be good."

"Great. Maybe give me an idea of when it'd be convenient for me to come, and I'll start looking at flights and places to meet."

"No worries, but I can't give you any dates yet. There's a contract I'm waiting to materialise. It's a big job, and I don't want to miss it. But I'll give you some dates soon."

And so, I hang on to the hope of seeing Adam. Because it sounds like our meeting might happen soon, I distance myself from James and begin to refuse sex. On the other hand, I press Adam for dates, but he doesn't budge, and I become short and sharp with him. For weeks on end, we go from gentle loving one minute, to remorseless fighting about seeing each other the next. He says he wants me to dump James first. I want to see him first to judge our compatibility before I make any drastic moves. A rolling barney.

One day, Adam drunk calls me. "I understand why you're so frustrated. You can't believe that a poor man like me, here in Africa, can say no to sex with a rich woman like you, in the UK," he chuckles and carries on, "I have a choice to say no you know. You can't force me to do it Zoro! You feminists are inconsistent. When it's you women, you call it harassment or rape when men force you, but when it's a man, what do you call that?" He releases a slow, malevolent guffaw.

"Does it bother you that I have money and you don't, Adam? I think we've talked about this before, but I think we should go over it again. Do you feel intimidated by my social status?"

"Of course not. I've been with all types of women, some richer and more beautiful than you! *Zvizukuru zvaShaka zvizegwe vuno!*" His words sting inside my chest.

"Ok, so why are you bringing money into justifying your patchiness? One minute you want us to meet, and one minute you don't. One minute you say you want to be with a married woman and the next, you don't. One minute you're sending me nudes, the next you're saying I'm pressuring you to have unwanted sex. What do you expect me to feel when you send me those pictures? When you text me messages of how you want to worship my naked body, and how you want to ravage me... What is the purpose of those communications, if not incitement to have sex at some point?"

Adam continues to spew fallacies about me in his drunken stupor, insinuating that I'm forcing him to have sex. Offended by his accusations, I tell Adam it's over and hang up on him.

DON'T YOU DARE

...be black,
successful
& woman,
because
a man will
find a reason
to break you

James has begun insisting that I travel with him on business trips. Now that I'm free of Adam, I join him on a trip to Rome. With relaxing warm weather and blooming Mediterranean florae - hibiscus, bougainvillaeas, yuccas, cacti and succulents that remind me of Zimbabwe - I feel at home there.

"*Ndozvaunodaka izvi* baby, *zvekudya nyika rutivi*," James says as we finish our scoops of pistachio gelato, our favourite Italian dessert. The atmosphere is convivial; we should be happy, but I'm not. "*Wagutaka nhasi,*" he goes on to say. The tone of his voice implies I should be grateful he allowed me to finish a generous helping of rich creamy carbonara and now, the privilege of pudding, without his usual denigrating running commentary.

Leave me alone for goodness sake, I want to say to him, but I focus on my ice cream and try not to think of Adam. I don't want to waste my time wondering why James resents the idea of pleasing my senses. I find it difficult to ignore the sarcasm in his voice when he adds, "Now that I'm being Mr. Romantic, maybe you can also write one or two poems about me."

I almost gust into laughter, thinking what horrible pieces I'd write about him. *Some things are best kept internalised.* He doesn't even look at me when he speaks. He's on his phone as usual, and I couldn't care less what he's doing on it. I want to tell him it's him I've always wanted, not the things he can buy me with money, but he has consistently denied me what I need and the time for such conversations is long gone. *I can't be begging for love from my own husband of over thirty years! I'm in my fifties now, for heaven's sake!*

HE'S FOUND LOVE?

From the corner of my eye
I observe him grinning at his phone,
vigorously drumming the screen with an eagerness
I've not seen in many years.

To my relief, unfamiliar emotions emanate—
Joy. Hope. Things I've not felt in a while:
this could well be my only way out. Freedom,
in whatever shape or form it comes… I'll take it
and so, I pray earnestly that he's found love.

Later on, I take a few pictures of James and I on an exclusive balcony of the cosy trattoria where we had our dinner. I post them on social media, citing a "Romantic getaway in Italy" to prove a point. Although I'm not sure to whom I'm proving what. *I love my husband?* But no matter how hard I try, I can't feel close to James, and I seem to loathe him more when I miss Adam. The foibles of his youth are also more apparent when I don't have Adam, each one with its own annoying personality and devilish head, brandishing monstrous long-nailed tentacles, causing me miscellaneous discomforts. I want to swat each head with a large garden spade, but I feel sorry for James. What would become of him without his baggage?

PRETENCE

> *Sometimes*
> *it's easier to pretend*
> *that the love is still there*
> *so you kiss, cuddle and hold hands*
> *in front of the kids and other participants*
> *but at night, you clench your buttocks and clutch*
> *onto the base of the bed to avoid rolling to the centre*
> *of the mattress where your intolerant behinds might touch &*
> *have that uncomfortable exchange they've been evading for years*

A day after my romantic exhibition, Adam sends me voice notes, weeping over his heartbreak and disappointment. I remind him that we're not together anymore, so I can do as I please. He refuses to leave me alone, and eventually I allow it.

James is out at an all-day conference and has left a wad of 500 Euro notes on the dressing table. I'm bored of shopping, so I've stayed put in our five-star hotel. I've had a warm à la carte brunch with a few glasses of prosecco mimosas, and I've been to the spa. I smell of ripe peaches, guavas and granadillas, after a facial treatment and full body massage with indulgent Mediterranean oils and creams.

I want Adam.

Back in our honeymoon suite, I'm lying naked on the king-size bed, gazing at a large bouquet of white peonies and scented garden roses placed at the centre of a Venetian, hand carved walnut table. The room is spacious, and the sunlight glowing through the sheer jacquard curtains makes beautiful patterns on the polished wooden floor. The allure of the room is intoxicating. I get up to fumble for Judah in the inner zipped pocket of my Louis Vuitton perched next to the flowers – it's my favourite designer handbag that I use on upper-crust trips to command respect.

The intricately carved bed matches the table, and it's dressed in luxurious linens in neutral colours. I get back on it and shuffle a bit to get comfortable, my eyelids closed to sharpen my perception. I can feel the speed and temperature of my blood rising with each breath, and I try to calm myself.

With Judah in my hand, I lie on my back until my body becomes deeply relaxed. I'm gagging for penetration, but I can't bring myself to insert the crystal wand into my vagina. My mind is fixated on Adam, with no other distracting thoughts. I take in deep breaths and exhale completely to rid my body of any residual tension from my massage earlier. As my mind and body begin to reach the sleep state, I can feel energy vibrating from Judah to envelop me with love and protection. I feel a tingling sensation in my toes, which begins to rise and spread throughout my body. I resist falling asleep by keeping my mind in a meditative state.

With my eyes still closed, and still thinking of Adam, I begin to visualise the ambrosial fruit havened between my thighs. At its core is the kaleidoscopic Eye of my I – the Shrine of my Ego. I see The Eye opening and closing, and my vagina pulsates in sync with its movements. It eventually opens wide and stays open, and I see a familiar human figure reflected in its pupil, at first very small, then he becomes larger and larger as he approaches. His form climbs out of The Eye and stands over me.

It's Adam. My Adam! We immediately recognise each other and I rise to meet him in a euphoric embrace. We unweave briefly to gape into each other's eyes, our fingers caressing then entwining to confirm this is all real. Our lips touch gently to find synchronicity, then lapse into a long passionate kiss. We fall onto the bed, feeling boundless joy.

Although there's a blurred line between my objective and astral realities, my senses are heightened and I can feel, hear and smell everything a hundredfold. A decadent fusion of scents - jasmine, white-edged frangipani and earth upon receipt of long-awaited rain - vaporises, and the sound of ethereal drums gently beats to ancestral humming. Our soft sighs increasingly fill the air and our hearts drum in sync with the beautiful music.

Adam's tongue caresses my erect nipples and the hairs on my skin stand taller than they've ever done. His hands, gentle like seraphic wings, part my legs wide open and he whispers, "You are the most beautiful woman in my world." I feel cocooned by the feathers of his love. When he nibbles the sides of my neck, I feel all my past traumas dissipating. I kiss him back and hold him desperately tighter. When he finally sinks into my succulent hole, we merge into one soul. We are complete.

The depth and intensity of our oneness surpasses anything experienced in the material world, and our spirits download and upload each other's feelings and thoughts. Each amorous caress and kiss is felt on a profound level, sending ripples of ecstasy through our beings. In surrender to the bliss of this timeless expression of pure connection, we become lost in the infinite depths of our love.

For hours and hours, we merge and remerge, waltzing to loops of the melody in our hearts until they blend into an explosive harmony—

I open my eyelids to the buzz of my phone. My body feels paralysed.

I can't decide whether I'm deeply relaxed or utterly exhausted, but I'm certainly heartbroken to be back in an Adamless reality. It's an unbearable solitude that makes me think about ending my own life. I'm drenched in sweat and can feel the delicious pain of coital friction between my legs. But

Judah is still clean and dry in my hand. Slowly, my ability to move returns. I drop Judah on the bed then touch myself to find an abundance of sticky wetness that can only happen when a man ejaculates repeatedly inside you. With cum dribbling down my legs, I run to check that the hotel room door is locked, and it is. James is still at work and Adam certainly is not here.

Tears begin to roll down my eyes as I become more and more alert to the disappointment and pain of my physical existence. I wail uncontrollably from the depth of my core until I suddenly remember that James might turn up any time and find me in this inexplainable state.

I jump into a cold shower where I begin to feel more refreshed and awake as fluids off my body flow into the drain with sudsy water.

Confused about what may have happened, I convince myself that I hallucinated or perhaps had a lucid dream. But my vagina, still swollen from prolonged intromission, is pulsating with remnant pleasure and still sensitive to touch. I walk out of the shower and dry myself, then remember my phone has been vibrating.

James is asking me to meet him for dinner at a nearby restaurant. I confirm I'll see him at 8pm. As we exchange these messages, I pause to ponder how we failed our relationship, or how it failed us. Could it be that our voices vanished with the arrival of our children? Not only did they silence our sounds of pleasure during love making, forcing artificial silence where it did not fit, but they also made us stop arguing and disagreeing, forcing us to maintain an illusion of perfection and bliss. As our communication dwindled, resentment quietly grew, until it began choking our union. I feel guilty blaming our children for our own shortcomings and quickly halt that stream of consciousness.

There are messages from work. I ignore those!

There's also a message from Adam. "Today, I feel like I'm with you physically. I can't explain it, but I think you know what I mean. It's the most beautiful thing. I love you, Zoro." I freak out again and the irrepressible thumps in my chest make me throw the phone into my bag without responding.

The next day, when I ask Adam to explain what he meant in his text, he doesn't answer my question. I decide to neither probe nor share my experience with him unless he brings it up first, or he might think I'm crazy. Especially because he has already suggested that I'm pressuring him to have unwanted sex!

By the time James and I return home in Herefordshire, Adam and I are properly back together. But, at every opportunity, Adam cites how much I hurt him. I tell him I was hurt too, by his callous accusations.

"I just want to say, we don't ever need to have real sex, or make love, or whatever you call it in your head. The feelings alone are good enough for me. To be able to yearn for it again, for me, is beautiful. Of course, a proper fuck would be equally beautiful. But to yearn for it forever might be even more beautiful. Imagine the poems of wanting I'll write for you from this deliberate creation of perpetual wanting." I say to Adam, although the truth is, I would give anything to experience him the way I did in Rome. I've had plenty erotic thoughts about him before, but the Italian encounter was otherworldly.

"I have feelings for you, and I fight them every day. That's the truth. I want you. That's the truth. All else is a result of my fight against this," he responds.

"I might just be at peace if we never do it in real life. I think we do it in my mind, I'm so tired. I wish I could stop the visions. It's as if I'm under a spell. I know I don't like sex enough in real life to think about it as much as I do. It's nuts!"

"This thing we're doing is not easy."

"I'm sorry our love is so complicated. You've offered me love and my broken self just hasn't known how to deal with it. I realise now that I've never had a proper courtship with the intention to just love. I got with James to get married and give him children. Now I'm like a child in the body of a fifty-year-old, jittery and confused. I'm sorry my love. From now on, I will be more intentional about what I do and say."

Due to James's increased travel, and him insisting that I accompany him, it becomes a bit more difficult for Adam and I to communicate freely, especially at night. So, I find a South African online liquor store and order four bottles of their finest whisky, delivered to Adam's door in Yeoville. That keeps him at bay for days. He posts his bottles on social media and on his WhatsApp status. And when he sobers up, we love each other with words.

Back in Herefordshire, I'm foraging for wild garlic leaves beneath a massive Monkey puzzle tree at the edge of our garden where it merges with the forest. My phone bleeps and I sit on a nearby felled tree stump to chat with Adam.

"Tell me again why you love me sweetie."

"I just do." I tell him, desperately.

"But I have nothing to give you."

"I don't want anything but your love Adam. Loving you has made me fall in love with life itself. Plus, I've always wanted to experience what else a man can offer, besides money and gifts."

"But I'm ghetto. I have issues!"

"*Ndokuda wakadero.* I want to feel real love with no frills. Besides, every time you tell me you're flawed, I think to myself 'who isn't?' We're all flawed… should the word 'flawed' even exist? If I'd had this understanding of humanness a long time ago, a lot of things that broke me in the past would have been insignificant."

"Sometimes I just think I'm not the guy you think I am. I can't give you what you want because I'm just a fuck up."

"I envy your life, your freedom," I can't help but open up.

"And I envy yours. You seem to have everything you want."

"Except that everywhere I go, I'm controlled and institutionalised. I'm also tired of being conscious of my blackness in this country. I wanna go back home."

"So why don't you?"

"It's complicated."

"Still, at least you have everything you want."

"I don't have you." I mean it when I say this, but he releases a brief, goofy laugh. "You know what, Adam, we've not always had money. We started off very poor. In fact, James and I met during a shift at a mushroom farm during our university years. And we struggled so much financially, as first-generation immigrants. But we decided back then that we'd work hard, doing whatever it took to never lack again. We could have decided to be fuck ups and remain stuck in a cycle of fuckery. You too can decide to stop being a fuck up. You can change your destiny, Adam. We hold on to our ancestral traumas and propagate negative patterns in order to stay faithful to our past. And we reinforce that sense of self by offloading our shit onto others. But that is so unnecessary. Stop passing on your negative drama to others, my love. You can decide that even if everyone else around you is poor, or a fuck up, you're going to break that pattern and be different. I'm saying this to show you I don't judge you based on what you have or don't have. I've experienced what you're going through."

"But you grew up rich."

"No, James grew up very poor, and mine was just a middle-class upbringing. My parents grew up in the ghetto and I still have relatives who live there."

"*Nhema dzako!* Where exactly?"

"*Ndorevesazve!* They're there *kwa*Mucheke *kwako ikoko*. My grandparents' house is *muna* Chechekunde Crescent – I have cousins living there now. I've got an uncle *muna* Calvin Majange Street, and an aunt *muna* Munyaradzi Vhudzijena. More cousins *muna* Mangwandi…"

"Wow, *saka* we're birds of a feather *zvomene*. Our house is *muna* Mboroma."

"You see, *handirevi nhema*. But even if we had grown up rich, I've still experienced being a poor economic refugee in a racist, classist country. Forced migration is not easy, and I too have suffered. But at the same time, money doesn't excite me. I treat the rich and the poor equally."

"Losing excitement over money. Romanticising poverty. I bet you listen to Bob Marley's song where he talks about his single bed and think, *I want a good fuck on a single bed.*"

"It's not that I think money is not important. It's just that I'm not obsessed with it. I don't allow having or not having it to define who I am, or to determine my level of happiness. I can be happy without it and sad when I have it."

"I see."

"I like to make the most of a bad situation. If electricity goes, for instance, while I understand the frustrations of that, I'd see it as an opportunity to be romantic, to put all gadgets away and bask in each other's presence, with scented candles burning in the background. After all, you have no control over some of these issues, so why not make the most of it? Does that mean I romanticise poverty?"

"You're curious about a life that you don't live, which isn't pleasant to those who live it."

"We are all different and I see people for who they are. Not where they are or how they're living their lives. And of course, if I start interacting with someone at a personal level, I become interested in how they live, in the same way they might be fascinated by how I live. I have experienced being poor and being comfortable – not rich – and I believe I can survive in both situations easily. And when I look back at my life, I was probably happier, or had less problems, when I had nothing. I used to think money would make me happy. I fought so hard to get to a point where I earned a lot of it and lost my mind during the process. Only to get there and realise I was still very unhappy – one of the reasons I found myself in therapy. How can I not lose interest in something that steals my joy? And look at me now, finding happiness in writing poetry! Something that doesn't cost me anything except time."

"*Ho nhai?*"

"What happened to treating all people like human beings, whether they're rich or poor? Us Zimbabweans have a complex *manje*. The tendency to only respect the rich or educated and looking down on the poor. That's nonsense!"

"You know I love you, right?"

"Yes, and I love you. I want to be with you."

"I will always, always love you Zorodzai. *Chimbondifonera* so I can hear your beautiful voice."

Later that evening, after speaking with Adam, I season and bake cubed salmon fillets parcelled in wild garlic leaves, punctuated by honey-soused feta and red peppers on steel skewers. When they're cooked and golden brown, I place the shish kebabs on a bed of fluffy brown rice. On the side is an avocado, chickpea and pomegranate salad embellished with chopped shallots, sundried tomatoes and broken marula seeds. There's nothing quite like a scrumptious meal to complement a delicious affair.

Around our tenth month of loving, Adam asks me to call him urgently. One of his contracts is taking longer than usual to pay out, and his rent is due.

"My love, this is very difficult for me. I don't usually ask people for..."

"Oh Adam, I'm not people! You're the love of my life."

"Thank you, my empress. *Eish,* so there's 5000 Rand for rent, then 300 for food, and..." I can tell he's accustomed to telling tales to make people loosen their pockets. Before he carries on with the discomforting calculations, I ask him for a total amount.

"How about 10,000 Rand?" Before the call is over, I send him a screenshot of the World Remit transaction confirmation.

"I promise to give you back every cent. I can do instalments or..."

"When you have it. Don't worry about it."

Adam works intermittently and makes sure to send me a picture of himself in a work suit and helmet whenever he's working. Sometimes he sends me foxy messages in the morning, and it makes me forget the questions that often bounce around in my head – like what he survives on when he spends most of his days on benders.

"Woke up horny sha. *Bhabharasi* makes me horny. So I was late for work, masturbating."

"OMG! You're not serious. Which photo did you use?"

"The one where you were straight out of the shower, water trickling down your full chest, steam rising from your chocolate skin."

"I'm relieved that after all this time, you still haven't replaced me."

"My love. I'm as lonely as my dick."

"You will tell me when you move on, won't you? I'd hate to deprive another woman of what belongs to her. I've been on the receiving end of it, and I'd never wish it on another woman."

"I will, IF I do."

We spend the rest of that day texting how much we miss each other, discussing how our first embrace and touch of lips will feel. "I know you don't have much experience in bed, because all you know is what your husband has taught you."

"And how do you know he hasn't taught me well?"

"If you find it embarrassing to fart, it means you have not farted during sex, which means you've not been fucked properly. I will ram into you until those sounds lose meaning to you." Adam goes on to sprinkle voice notes in my phone, telling me how much he longs for me, how much he wants to kiss me. He says it from his core, with a slight stammer, injecting a palpable energy of desire into me.

I'm sitting in the garden with a cup of syrupy rooibos tea, savouring the early morning sun and imagining him and me in a playful 69, teasing each other's perinea with the tips of our tongues, until my sweet daydream is abruptly interrupted by Peter screaming "the biscuits are gone!", as if to absolve himself of any responsibility of finishing the said biscuits. When the *disaster* is resolved, I return to my phone.

A waking voice whispers,
I am his decadent dessert
Warm and wet in the middle
Like the gooey centre of an
M&S melt-in-the-middle sponge:

Sometimes, "Deliciously soft and velvety chocolate pudding made with an
oozing Belgian chocolate sauce centre."
Other times, "A meltingly moist all butter chocolate sponge made with
almonds drenched in a sumptuous chocolate fudge sauce."
Or, "Chocolate pudding with a hidden centre of shimmering orange
flavoured sauce. Comes with a sachet of extra sparkle for you to sprinkle
over."

And my down below,
Sultry and sensuous
Dances the shimmy 'til it oozes
Food of the gods
—a wanton last course

"Zoro, what's this?" he adds several laughing emojis.

"I'm crazy about you Adam," I reply, then send him links to my favourite Marks and Spencer food adverts from which I extracted the quotes in my poem.

"The food looks amazing," he says after watching the adverts on YouTube.

"Everything they make is amazing. I'll send you some of their candy when I send you the books you asked for." When I do my grocery shopping, I buy Adam champagne chocolate truffles, Percy Pigs, gourmet jelly beans and other stuff to try, then courier the gifts to Yeoville.

Inside the parcel, I've included a fragranced handwritten letter, sealed with a red kiss.

Mudiwa Adam,

I don't remember the last time I hand-wrote a letter. A love letter for that matter. But the opportunity to send these sweet things roused the desire in my fingers to scribe a note to you. This might only happen once, and that thought excites me.

Anyway, how rude of me to not ask – Makadiiko Mukanya? Ini ndinobgwaira. So, I'm sitting at my desk, wearing a tie & dye linen kaftan.

When I lift my head, I see the garden beyond the double glass doors. There's a pebble-mosaic patio immediately after the French doors, just before a small area laid to lawn. A rustic octagonal sandstone birdbath sits on that small patch, where every morning, different types of birds come to cleanse themselves. Wrens, doves, bluebirds, robins, you name it. It's beautiful to observe them enjoying their freedom. Even on the coldest mornings, when the water in there is icy they bath in it anyway, which I find fascinating. Later in the day, when the birds are not there, I look at the bench where I sit when I speak with you sometimes. From the bench, I see lovely fat sheep grazing on nearby farmland – I can't see them from where I am right now. I recently bought a bird feeder – a sculptured squirrel with an open mouth, where I leave the bird food. It's placed inside the matching bird bath, so I can see the birds snacking throughout the day. I haven't had time to replace the food, so the feeder is empty, and the birds are currently as scarce as hen's teeth.

I love sitting here thinking about you, and what our future holds. I guess it's worth mentioning that before the doors that lead into the garden are a couple of large green foliage plants – a Monstera and a Xanadu. They give me lots of positive energy. Just looking at them makes me so happy, especially as fronds of new leaves unfurl when I least expect them to – it reminds me of how our love emerged…so suddenly, so fast and unexpected, yet delightful. To my right is a door that leads to the main lounge. I often imagine you walking in here from there to ask me if I'd like another cup of tea. I say yes, and you go and make me one in the kitchen, which is to my left, after the dining room. But I never get to drink the tea you make, because when you bring it, we kiss profusely and end up fucking on the green leather chesterfield sofa behind me. The one I place your things on when I take pictures I send to you. Okay, I probably shouldn't be writing naughty things in here.

I miss you. A lot. I've not yet got my head around the concept of missing someone I've never met. Isn't it strange, the love we feel for each other? Its depth – I find it fascinating. I can spend hours on end playing in my head, over and over, how it'll feel embracing you, holding hands and feeling each and every line in your palm, looking into each other's eyes, kissing, whispering "I love you". These thoughts must release a whole bunch of happy hormones into my body, and perhaps it is these hormones that make it possible to miss you so much and love you despite the odds of ever meeting. I have never felt love this deep before, and I don't ever want it to stop. Well, we have sometimes spoken about "the painful end" but I cannot imagine it. So I don't think about it, despite knowing it might happen. I'd rather live in the moment and enjoy the joy your love brings. And even if we go through the painful end, I will always love you. I don't know why.

I look forward to our union in the flesh. I would have wanted it to happen sooner, but life seems to have got in the way. Our fears also seem to be in the way. But that's ok. Love is patient, they say. I'm also learning to put into practice the other adage, that if you love someone you set them free.

A few days later, I paint my nails red, take a picture and send it to Adam.

"I know it's not the greatest paint job, but I wanted to feel cute today because I'm celebrating."

"Celebrating what?"

"I finally quit Tim. I sent him a message today and told him I am well enough and don't need therapy anymore."

"So why do you always have to put yourself down?"

"What do you mean?"

"That disclaimer. Why can't you just send the picture without mentioning that it's ugly? Your low self-esteem is annoying! Clearly, you don't love yourself!"

"What? It is factual that the paint job is shabby. I've had my nails done by a professional many times before and my eyes do not deceive me; the way I've done it isn't as nice as the nail technician does it! This has nothing to do with my self-esteem! And even if it does, the things I've gone through in life got me here. A victim is a victim because they've been victimised! I think you take our backgrounds and upbringings for granted."

"No, what you take for granted is my association with you. You're on your own now!"

"What do you mean?"

"I'm tired of how you put up with nonsense in your life, and I have to constantly lift you up. I know you've been through stuff in your life, but you identify with your past so much, like when will you grow out of it? I'm not replacing your therapist, Zoro. You're on your own comrade!"

"??????"

"You have been paying for therapy for years and this guy Tim loses nothing from your continued lack of belief in yourself. He actually benefits. Meanwhile, I need positive energy, so I'm sorry Zoro, you need someone who went to school to deal with your sort of problems. It definitely needs someone you pay. Someone who wants you to believe it takes as many years as it took to break you, to find yourself, as if you didn't already know yourself."

"So you've given up on me? From now on I'll say nothing about myself, I guess. And we can focus on just you. That way, we're both safe. I don't contaminate your positive energy and I don't feel let down."

"I'm not giving up on you. It has worked or not worked up to this point. I've just reached saturation, I guess. I am the tough-love kind of lover that your soul needs. I think that's the best kind of love I can give you at the moment."

"You make it sound like I haven't made any progress in my life, yet I've worked so hard to get to where I am. Do you know how tough it is to decide that I'm going to face my demons head-on and do whatever it takes to be mentally well? While others are trying to escape theirs by partying and drinking every day, I've been addressing my problems sober... after years of falling asleep drunk, I loved myself enough to stop, until I met you..."

"*Mhaka dzaani?*"

"*Tibvigwe!* For me to be able to do something as simple as write a social media post after the things I've been through, to share my pieces of writing that hundreds of people love. To quit therapy in itself is huge progress! Most of my social anxiety is gone, but you've just taken me a few steps back. Only I know my journey, and you're right, I shouldn't burden you with it."

"We can continue talking about things as we normally do, Zoro."

"Talk about what exactly? What's left to talk about *nhai*, because we've eliminated a lot, for the sake of your mental health. The more we talk, the more I dig a deeper hole for myself, the more I seem to be this horrible person who saps your energy, yet when we first 'met' you were all over *my* positive energy. You've sapped it all up haven't you, and I wish I'd never opened up to you about anything! You suck!"

My whole chest is searing and I'm in tears, now wondering if I've made the right decision leaving therapy. I had hoped it would be the first step towards mental independence and my detachment with the UK. If I could make it without Tim, I would go and live happily ever after in South Africa. But Adam's reaction makes me think if I leave James first, like he is insisting, he might react exactly like he has done now, and tell me I'm on my own. I resolve that on this basis, I will not leave James. I decide to never speak to Adam again. That night, with a bottle of gin on my bedside, I grieve. For Tim, for Adam and the whole mess I've managed to put myself in.

The next day, Adam sends me his ghetto apology, "I'm a fuck up." He thanks me for my beautiful letter which has just arrived - "its energy is palpable", and the delicious sweets - "they're very moreish". I smile but don't respond and turn to my poetry manuscript instead.

~~PROTESTING COLLUDER~~

~~*I love that we're together n shit*~~
~~*I know you think I'm the shit*~~
~~*Yet sometimes you act like I ain't shit*~~
~~*Breaking my little heart n shit*~~
~~*Then you say you're sorry n shit*~~
~~*Do you really ever mean*~~
~~*that shit*~~
~~*Now listen to me you little shit*~~
~~*You're now in such deep shit*~~
~~*Cause if you don't stop this shit*~~
~~*I'm gonna stick your face in shit*~~
~~*Don't say I didn't warn you n shit*~~

TRYING TO BREAK A CAUSTIC LOVE BOND

```
                    so   .                how to
        destroyed        .      me         stop
           nor              . Tell        loving
         created                            you
      neither be                            and
       that can                           I will,
        energy                              but
           is                            darling
          love                            please
      philosophies...                     don't
                        love          bore
                       your    me
        be      l             me   with  y
      to              o           hurt        o
   how                 v      You             u
   know                e                      r
    I                 d—by...            violence;
   way                                      I
   only                                    was
   the                                  raised by
      is                                 trauma,
       it                                   so
   because                              your
        more,                         cruelty
          you                        only
        love           makes
               me
```

After three weeks of trying hard to end it for good, I find myself sending Adam a message, telling him I miss him. He hasn't been seen on WhatsApp for over a week, so I send him messages on all his social media mailboxes.

"I've been trying very hard to stop loving you, but I can't. Or maybe I'm not trying hard enough. The harder I try, the stronger the feelings become. I don't know what has possessed me, I feel like I have completely lost control of myself. I feel sick when we don't communicate. Maybe I'll burn out…you know, get tired of you. The difficulty for me is being unable to express how I feel to you. It's a strange place to be, especially at my age. My heart hurts so bad, such an unfamiliar pain, sometimes I'm convinced it'll kill me in my sleep. But I won't burden you further with all this, so I'll stop here."

I get a response three days later.

"It's good that you have poured your heart out. It's not easy for me either, believe me. I don't know what is right and what is wrong. I've been waiting for it to burn out, conflictingly waiting for you to get fed up with me. I hate it when it's awkward between us." I hate it when he starts philosophising. "I will be offline till month-end. My phone fell into the toilet under mysterious circumstances, and I only got to know of it when the music in my EarPods stopped. I don't know how that happened. So, I'm having to log onto social media via Internet Explorer to check messages from a computer at work."

"Should I send you one of my iPhones? I have a couple just sitting here in my drawer, the contracts having expired, and I got replacements. It can be there in three days by DHL."

"No! I hate iPhones and everything that the Apple company stands for." He immediately forwards to me a Twitter thread discussing the Apple child labour scandal.

"Ok. How much is a new phone, Adam?" With the month-end being three weeks away, I've got to do something!

"My phone was an A32 and I want to upgrade to an A73 or A53. I'm trying to contact the Samsung service centre to see if I can salvage anything from my water damaged phone. I bought it for 5000 Rand, but I expect far much less if there should be a trade in. The A73 is around 8500 Rand at Vodacom and just over 9000 Rand at Samsung and Takealot. I just want to improve, one step back, two steps forward." I recognise the pocket-loosening storytelling and send him 10,000 Rand to buy a new phone. And our love is back online, Adam telling me honey-drenched words that make me love him even more.

"I will pay you back, sweetness. Things are just not working out for me at the moment, but I promise you… maybe I can even do some jobs for you babe. If you have admin, or things like that. I can work for you until the debt is paid."

"Oh, there's no need for all that Adam."

After a year of loving Adam, I'm now quite comfortable with the idea of having an affair. In fact, I no longer feel like I'm cheating on James – I'm just living my life, as he is living his. I tell Adam about all my life problems, and he laughs them off as nonsense, but in an affectionate way, and his perspectives on life give me some respite.

"Let them cook and do the dishes for a change, Zoro. When does that lot ever do anything for you?" I love it when he empowers me this way, because I struggle to let go of my cycle of routine, especially when all children are home during the holidays. Adam can't believe I still drive my "grown up" kids to meet with their friends, even when it's raining.

"Let them walk! A little water never killed anyone…" he barks into the phone when I tell him I have to go and pick them up. "You never listen to me Zoro. Listen to me *mhani*!"

"Well, John's boyfriend, Tarquin is around. It wouldn't look good to not ferry them when the car is just parked there."

"What kind of name is *Takwini? Ha mazita eikokovo!*" he releases a prolonged laugh before stopping abruptly to say, "Boyfriend, as in *chikomba?*"

"Well, yes they're dating."

"*Aaaah! Ngito!* And your Zimbabwean husband knows this? Are you guys ok upstairs?"

"Adam, whether we like it or not, John will do what he wants anyway. He can either do it secretly or openly. I love that he trusts us enough to be open about his life choices."

"*Haaa zvechingochani bodo zve!*"

"Adam! Don't you ever call my son *ngito* or *ngochani* again *kana uchiri kuda nezvangu.* I will always love my son regardless of his sexual orientation."

"*Eish! Ngaisiye matambo horaiti. Chete ndinobva kughetto kune maelders.*" We agree to let it rest. We have become content with each other's shortcomings. We've had numerous fights and made up and feel like we've been married for years.

A few months later, the issue of meeting up comes up again. This time, Adam says he wants to meet, but he wants a concrete sign of commitment from me.

"I'll commit if you commit to me Zoro."

"I will leave him, I promise."

"I don't want you to leave your husband for me Zoro."

"You've changed your tune!"

"Well, imagine every time we fight, and you say, 'I left my marriage for you.' I don't want that Zoro. If staying is an option for you, then it's your decision, not mine."

"You will tell me if you've moved on, won't you?" He avoids the question.

"Can we schedule a call?" he says.

"Are you sober, Adam?" I know he's drinking when he doesn't answer the question.

"When the electricity comes back, we need to talk." We agree to speak later but continue texting in the meantime.

"What are you doing right now?" I ask whilst tidying up what might just be my first poetry manuscript.

"I'm playing my all-time favourite, *Mbwende* by Jah Prayzah, whilst finishing off this litre." He's drinking cheap whiskey.

"Wish I was there to dance with you." I reply, now wondering how he's playing music on his phone but can't speak due to his dying phone battery.

"I have two left feet, but *ndatombotamba ipapa*."

"Would you still have me as your wife?"

"Yes, but this question is too late, I think." My heart stops beating.

"Is this your way of telling me you've found a new lover?" My body temperature has shot through the roof.

"No. It's my way of telling you that I can't wait for you."

"Do you want to see me though?"

"I love you Zoro. I want to see you, without a doubt. This is my promise."

"Good. I think we should park all decision-making until we meet. I just might not bother coming back to the UK... You only tell me you love me when you're drunk though, Adam. You're annoying!"

"So, what does that mean to you?"

"It doesn't matter what it means to me. I want to hear it when you're sober, and when I feel like hearing it. And when I know you know I feel like hearing it."

"I want you to listen when I speak. Be my wife. Forget about patriarchy. Forget about your own ego. You can't do that?"

"I can do that only if I'm loved right."

"Can you be my wife?" I cringe, realising now how much I yearn to live and love freely, with no man-made prisons stifling my joy. I've experienced first-hand how quickly the excitement of love dwindles after marriage, and I won't be stupid enough to put myself through it again. The time I've known Adam has been great, but it has often brought my spirit down too. I don't want to be stuck in that world. But...

"I can be."

"I like this simple answer."

"You taught me simple. See. I listen."

"I think you love me."

"Of course I do."

"I want to see you Zorodzai. Only if you will be my wife – in private."

"What do you mean 'be your wife in private'?"

"Fair question. I don't know."

"I think you do. Tell me in simple terms what you want."

"I just said it cause it sounded cool."

"Well, in my heart, you're my husband. I love only you."

"This is the most beautiful thing you've ever said to me."

"I mean it."

"I know it." When the electricity comes back in South Africa, we speak non-stop for five hours, until he passes out, drunk. I go to sleep contented and fulfilled.

This time we've agreed to meet in Joburg. I book a flight for immediately after Peter finishes writing his A-Level exams. I will visit Adam at his home in Yeoville for two weeks. I plan to tell James I'm going on a business trip for one week, then meet with my friends for another week, for the reunion we cancelled a year and a half ago.

At this point, my life revolves around chasing Adam and waiting for his fawning responses when he feels like it. However, I'm intoxicated by his energy – something about him makes it impossible to let him go. He keeps giving like a well-fed potted orchid, with some periods of no bloom, but always giving pleasurable blossoms when the time is right.

"I'll never get used to your silent exits, Adam…it's like Zim parents who don't say hello or goodbye on phone calls. You pick up, they say what they want quickly and then hang up with no warning, Lol! I missed you all day today and I know I'm going to miss you tomorrow. I know I've said this before, but isn't it weird, missing someone you've never met? Anyway, speak soon."

the gentle crunch
of baby feet tiptoeing
on a sandy beach

the tickle of a ladybird
crawling up my thigh
on a summer's day

the breeze rousing
goosebumps— a spirit
walking through me

"Sorry for the silent exits. The thing is this, living by oneself is lonely. I'm in bed, chatting with you and then I sleep. Sometimes I wake up on top of my phone..." Adam replies two days later.

One morning, I find a meeting invite from my boss, asking me to be chaperoned by a colleague, as the meeting may result in the termination of my employment. I chuckle to myself and accept the invitation. For a very long time, I've not bothered to move the mouse on my desk to keep Microsoft Teams showing me as active when I'm not working. Quite often, when I send Adam a sulky selfie captioned "crap day at work", he says, *"ndifonere ndimboku softa"*, and I cancel all my meetings with no explanation, then go to perch on the sofa to be serenaded with words that make me giggle and blush until I'm exhausted. *"Kungohwa hwi rako so, yodomira,"* is the first thing he says, and I never get tired of hearing him saying how my voice turns him on.

The following day, my boss, Kevin, appears alongside the HR director and expresses concerns over my poor performance in the past year and how I've dismally failed to meet any of my work objectives. It doesn't help that I stopped attending their performative team building lunches and poxy Friday night drinks. I haven't been interested in office politics since I went part time.

"Do what you must Kevin," I respond nonchalantly. "I'm going through a lot currently and I can't change the way I conduct myself for you."

"Would you like me to organise support for you Zorodzai? Counselling maybe? Anything you need," the HR director interjects, shocked by the attitude of what used to be their high-flyer before I self-demoted a few years ago.

"No thanks! To hell with your capitalism, racism and sexism! When the whites are being incompetent, do you have such meetings with them? If I was a middle-aged white man, would we be here right now? I'm leaving this sad cold country. For good! To write poetry for the rest of my days!" Kevin and the HR director look at each other, gobsmacked, and thank me for my time. My employment ends. I say nothing to James.

In the meantime, Adam and I start online viewings of apartments in Cape Town, where we'll spend the rest of our lives doing it every day like a pair of bonobos.

We'll visit Cape Town to see potential homes during my visit. I'm not sure if I'll return to the UK, so I withdraw half my life savings, £30,000 from my ISA, then send Adam an image of the cash and bank withdrawal slip as my sign of commitment. I'm going with the wind and the future looks bright.

A month before my trip, Adam disappears for five days, and although I frantically text and try to call him at first, I eventually relax and wait. I've become accustomed to who he is. Eventually, he responds, "I don't really have an interest in life, or anything related, of late."

"I hate everything about life too. And like you, I think about death a lot. But I think there's a good reason why our paths crossed; two people with all these things in common. I don't have the right words to make you feel better, as I sometimes fail myself, but all I can give you is my love and support, and hope that it somewhat gives you a (small) reason to want to carry on. Well, sometimes it's not even about wanting to carry on, but the responsibilities we carry. The people who want you to live. The things we're doing to change the world. You're in a vicious cycle and alcohol makes the depression worse due to inflammation. You feel sad and you drink. The depression gets worse due to inflammation, and you drink more to make yourself feel better. And the cycle continues. And you have been doing the most with alcohol lately, so I'm not surprised things are so bad at the moment."

Adam responds the next day, "Thank you," then calls me a few hours later.

When I answer the phone, he is as drunk as a skunk and begins to lecture me about my "colonised mind".

"Your type doesn't even know the difference between equity and equality! Toxic feminis…"

"Excuse me?"

"And you think that living in a nice house in a good neighbourhood will save you from racism! You think all those white people you interact with on Twitter genuinely like you? No white person will ever truly love or appreciate a black person, Zoro."

"So, you want me to go and live in places where my own people will rob me of my hard-earned things when I can afford to be somewhere I can forget to lock my front door? Places where my daughter can go for an evening stroll on her own and return home in one piece?"

"*Haiwavo*, you're colonised!"

"*Nyangwe newevo*, you're just as colonised, if you claim to believe in Shona spirituality but you can't even explain how you practise your beliefs! *Heee* venerating ancestors, *heee* respecting ancestors – but how do you do it? It's no wonder Christians are always denigrating your African spirituality!" I taunt him, then quickly realise my digression. "Listen, white supremacy is not my problem, Adam. It's a white people's issue that they may or may not be aware of. Either way, it's on them to sort themselves out, not me. Meanwhile, I don't have the time and energy to hate them while they fix themselves. Or not. Life's too short for histrionics."

"Whites will never be good to you..."

"You're more racist than the whites, Adam..."

"Impossible! Blacks can never be racist..."

"Oh please..."

"Look at me here struggling in South Africa. It was the white man who designed this, by making alcohol cheap and accessible to the black man, so that when he's exhausted by capitalism, he'll drink during his free time and go back to work, never having free time to think of other things...how to develop himself."

"If you know the system is designed to trap you, don't play the game then! You could always choose to not bite the bait, Adam." I try to interject but no one hears me. "Ok, different angle. How can we end capitalism?"

"I don't know."

"So why do we bother making so much noise about it? Why don't you work towards getting rich yourself so you can stop coming across as jealous of people who've earned their wealth. Not everyone who's rich is a capitalist; you do know that don't you?"

"Do you understand capitalism, Zoro? Your own husband is a capitalist, and you don't even know it! You're delusional my love..."

"Enough already!" I hang up on Adam and switch off my phone. I'm left so shaken, I consider cancelling my trip. The next day, when I've played the conversation over and over in my mind, I send Adam a message.

"You can lecture me all you like about oppressive systems, but one thing you can never do is teach me to hate people. Same way I hate the patriarchal system but can love an individual man who is good to me. My guiding principle in life is love. That is what makes me choose to see the best in people, even the ones you think should be hated simply because they are beneficiaries of a system that disadvantages you. I apply myself consistently in my dealings with human beings, regardless of who they are. I will not return negativity. I will neutralise it with love instead. And those who want to use up their energy hating can do so. You choose to see the worst in people, even those who have done good to you. I'm not sure what you gain from it, but it must bring you some sort of pleasure. Personally, I feel that it takes great effort to hate, to constantly be scouring for something bad in people must be exhausting. No one is perfect, me and you included. So why choose the bad instead of the good? Other than souring relations and depriving yourself of opportunities, what do you stand to gain from it?"

"I'm not going to read all of this because I wasn't teaching you to hate individuals."

"I'm not coming there anymore Adam."

"Talk to me Zoro. Why would you make such a drastic decision?"

"I can sense that you're not into me anymore."

"That's not the case my love." He lapses into philosophical explanations about the complexity of our relationship. It would also seem awkward to James, cancelling the trip out of the blue like that. Plus, Adam and I are already planning a life together. Surely, he's only acting up because he's lacking the direction of a strong woman. And this is also precisely the sort of turbulence that is described by spiritual scripts on the twin flame phenomenon. I will have to see it through because I don't want to return to this world in another lifetime to learn the life lesson Adam is destined to teach me. I settle on seeing it through.

Three weeks before my journey, Adam sends a message saying he has a new contract with a big company based in a small town called Lephalale, in Limpopo.

"My love, I can't refuse the kind of money they are offering me here."

"Should I cancel the trip then? What about Cape Town?"

"No. You can still come, and we'll see each other when I'm not working shifts. The shifts are pretty long though. 7am to 7pm."

"So, you want me to come there to spend 12-hour days on my own?"

"I can make some sacrifices when you get here. My team understands. And the boss is my friend."

"After those long shifts, surely you'll have no energy left to even take off my underwear."

"You're fucking with the wrong nigga!"

"Ok, how do I get there?"

"I'll take a day off to come and pick you up from the airport. Failing that, you can catch a Sprinter, but it shouldn't come to that."

"What's a Sprinter?"

"They are Mercedes minibuses, bigger than a kombi, but smaller than a bus. They come here from Joburg all the time."

"I need to get my head around this. I've Googled where you are, and it seems very remote."

"I can give you an unforgettable experience in the unlikeliest of places, Zorodzai. What you don't realise is that you saved me from myself. And for that, I want to worship you."

LOVE IN LIMPOPO

After two whole days of silence
I'm convinced he is dead,
as I do when he's been at it,
but the proof of life pings on my phone & it reads:
I'm working in Limpopo

Oh, my love, why do you
sprinkle our lives with such disarray,
as if our love is not prismic enough?
He wants me to go and see him there,
in Limpopo

What choice do I have?
I love him, but we've never met,
and he's the love of my life.
Where is this going? My inner voice asks
and my gut submits, I'm going to Limpopo

Excited to finally meet Adam, I go through the gift buying rituals and sprucing myself up for "the match." This time, I order three personalised Arsenal football shirts from the last and present seasons in all varieties of his totem clan names – Makwiramiti, Vhudzijena, Shoko. I buy him the finest whiskies and little things he's mentioned he likes, as well as medium-sized acrylic on canvas original paintings of Tupac, Thomas Sankara and Che Guevara, signed by the artists. I send him pictures of the gifts, and he replies, "those things are to me what peanut butter is to rats." He sends me online links to the anti-imperialist revolutionary speeches of Sankara that he has sent me before. I put my earphones on and beam as I bubble wrap his gifts and ruminate… *we'll soon hang these up in our beachfront house in Cape Town, where I'll write poems and run a small restaurant serving Zimbabwean cuisine, for the rest of our days.*

LEPHALALE

The word sounds beautiful…Lephalale
So I look up its meaning—"to flow"
in Setswana.

There's a river that flows through Lephalale
alongside tributary streams of the Limpopo
and that makes me glow, for I am a river goddess
and as the gods will have it, only the flow of true love
can lure me there

I suddenly realise there will be no time for Adam to get tested for HIV, and there's no point in me getting tested again. As I'm wondering how to resolve this, I come across a Facebook post on PrEP. I'm pleasantly surprised by this medical advancement and immediately Google where I can find it in the UK, other than my family GP. I learn that PrEP can be ordered at any pharmacy, so I drive into town the next day and enter Boots. There is a black woman behind the counter. When I queue up, I notice the name on her badge is Zimbabwean and retreat to the cosmetic aisle where I pace up and down, pretending to browse, until the Zimbabwean disappears, replaced by a white woman.

I go back to the counter and ask if they sell PrEP. The woman says she has never heard of it before, so she calls the resident pharmacist, a man of Asian origin. Even he has never heard of it. I retrieve my phone and show the man the different articles about PrEP on Google. Intrigued by this new information, the pharmacist takes some details down and says he'll look into this exciting drug. I end up ordering a few months' supply of PrEP from an online pharmacy then immediately begin to self-medicate.

WHAT THE GODS INTENDED

Nothing has happened as planned

for us—is our love cursed?

Am I supposed to be coming

to you, in Limpopo?

But where else could such a volcanic union happen,

where else? Everything is as the gods intended.

So, I am coming to you

and will be coming with you

—in Limpopo.

The preparation routine I've created makes the impending trip feel more real than ever. The large blue pills I struggle to swallow daily begin to make me feel dizzy and nauseous, but I'm willing to do whatever it takes to be with Adam.

100

I'M GOING TO LIMPOPO

I've made my mind up

I'm going to Limpopo

to worship the god in my dreams

—he seems real

but I have to go and see for myself

that I haven't made him up in my head.

Nothing makes sense

except to be with him.

The visions in my head

flood my conscious with desire

But what will we do when I get to Limpopo

when I've found and embraced him?

Adam becomes less available as my departure date draws closer. He explains that he's working twelve-hour shifts, and there's very bad mobile reception at his lodge in Lephalale.

"I don't think I'll get any time off while you're here, so you'll be bored."

"*Hino zvohumwi?* Anyway, I'll figure out stuff to do on my own while you're at work." After this conversation, which we've had before, Adam says, in addition to working long hours, sometimes he's out drinking, or he is sleeping long hours due to exhaustion. Sometimes, his phone is out of charge due to loadshedding. But, no matter what, he communicates eventually. And that standard becomes the norm for me.

I send him a message at 8.05pm
to say I'm going to take a nap
just in case he sends me a message
while I'm asleep and wonders
why I'm taking too long to respond.

We're going through a mending phase
where our "I love you's"
are far and few between

but I love him deeply right now and
I badly want to tell him
that should I not wake
from my nap,
I want him to know
he's the best I've ever had.

"*Chimbondisofta sha,*" I ask Adam to furnish me with sweet nothings.

"It's not too romantic when the migrant worker is tired from a 12-hour shift."

"Yet you claim you'll ravage me after the same 12-hour shift?" I'm sipping from a champagne flute to ease my mind.

"Well, maybe I can't and it's just masculinity speaking. It's not like I have a reference point."

Okay. I love you and it hurts that I don't know how you feel about me anymore. I wish your coldness would make me fall out of love with you. I really do. But there's a fey force behind my feelings for you...something I simply can't control no matter how hard I try. I might just cry myself to sleep... My thoughts are running wild.

He is busy with work
As I am busy with zing
I want to build up to this…
The wait has been long.
But he has no energy
And must keep working,
So I talk to myself, at him
Hoping he might ignite
The spark that makes
All of this make sense
But I have doubts
About his promise made once
Of an experience I will not forget.
My heart is swollen with want
And perhaps it will explode
—To set me free

One day when Adam is off shift, he gets drunk and sends me pictures of himself. He's been ignoring most of my love messages over the last few days, only cherry picking a few to respond to.

"You hate me! Unless you're shit drunk and hating yourself, you don't miss or love me. Or at least you can't say how you feel about me."

"*Ko izvozvo wazviwanepi?* Isn't this a bit dramatic Zoro? Of course it can't be the same. As you know, I have to put my mental health first. I am happier and my love is a bit animated when I'm drunk, but you can't always follow up on a message I missed to raise a point. Feels like your messages were a set up. You can say what you want to say without setting up a grand stage to say it. It's unfair and a little disheartening."

"In a relationship where we don't see each other and don't speak every day, the least you can do to make me feel wanted and loved is to say words of affirmation. But your mental health matters so much, you're allowed to be weird at the expense of mine. If you can't regularly say how you feel about me in the kind of relationship we have, one has to wonder why we are in it in the first place. I don't think questioning this is being dramatic at all. I want to feel loved every single day. That is all I ask and that is precisely why I'm here. If this is too much to ask, then I don't know what to tell you." I immediately send him another message. "Sorry you hate it when I express my feelings. I've told you how much I miss you since our last voice conversation. You've literally just ignored all of those messages. You're already disheartened. I don't need to do or say anything to get you there."

"It's just how you say these things, Zoro. Plus, when I'm sober, I'm consumed with the guilt of being with a married woman. Does it not bother you Zoro?"

"Not anymore. I no longer look at life that way. No one owns anyone. The institution of marriage is one of ownership – owning women like commodities and treating them anyhow because they're paid for. I can't conform to that anymore. I love you and I'm not going to feel guilty for being with the man I love. That's it."

"Yeah, but after making love with me, you will return to your husband and I'll be left with the guilt of having done it, forever."

"Ok, if having sex is such a big issue, why don't we just not have it? We've discussed this before, and you know this relationship is bigger than sex. I'll book a hotel room where I'll stay on my own, and we can meet somewhere neutral and public when you're not working."

"Is that even possible?"

"Of course! All we need to do is agree that we won't do it, and actually mean it. If I can go for two years with no alcohol, trust me, I can be in the same bed as you and not succumb to sex. Remember– willpower." He does not respond, and I mix gin tipples to quell my frustration.

"Are we still trying not to fuck?" he responds a day later.

"I guess we could if you want to. We definitely should." I decide to respond with what I think Adam wants to hear, then change the subject. "Let's play it by ear when I get there. I've been checking out excursions in Limpopo. I'd really like to visit Mapungubgwe. Can you let me know when you're not working so I can book a safari tour for both of us?"

"Ok, right now I don't know what my working hours will be when you come. I'll let you know."

I go ahead and book my accommodation in Lephalale on Airbnb.

VOICES IN HIS HEAD

it is when the voices
in his head
are muted by spirits
that his heart unbolts
and his mouth opens
to say he loves me

A few days before my flight, I send Adam a voice note in an imitation of Loretta Devine's voice, to tease him, asking whether he wants my down below waxed or woolly. Adam replies with a salivating emoji and we spend all morning deliberating the pros and cons of each option. I chicken out on wax and decide to shave myself instead.

With my heart palpitations out of control with excitement, not even breathing exercises can calm me down. Over the years, I've worked hard to slow my mind, and I cannot believe how easily I was lured onto Adam's turbulent rollercoaster. I send an urgent message to Michelle, pleading for a reiki session. Luckily, there's been a cancellation and Michelle can see me the next morning.

I whizz through the rush-hour traffic in anticipation of some spiritual healing. I'm elated that even at the busiest intersections, all traffic lights are green, allowing me to make it on time for my appointment at 9am.

Michelle is pleased to see me after what seems like a lifetime. We share a comforting cuddle and exchange pleasantries. Then Michelle instructs me to recline on the massage table, close my eyes, and take deep breaths. She begins to walk around the bed, brandishing a burning white sage smudge stick. When it burns out, she places her warm hands on my chest and speaks in a gentle, hypnotic voice, "Imagine the crown of your head opening and let the stream of healing white light flow from the top of your head, into your heart, and out through your arms and hands. Allow it to fill and surround you, completely cleansing and purifying your mind, body and spirit." I immediately become unconscious.

An hour later, Michelle calls me back from my astral travel.

"Wow! That was amazing! You left your body the whole time. For a moment, I thought you might not come back." Michelle is hot and flushed, despite having been standing with her palms on my body the whole time. "I've never felt such an overflow of love in one's heart before. Spirit led me to your heart and that's the energy centre I focused on today. I had to shift the energy from that chakra to your solar plexus and your throat chakras, to create balance and harmony in your body. You are healed, my darling." I take a few moments to gather my bearings before I'm able to speak.

"Thank you, my lovely. I have no recollection of anything, but I feel soothed and restored, like I went into a deep sleep I've not experienced before."

"You had interesting chaperones too, and it was quite an experience for me."

"Chaperones?"

"Yes. Raphael was here. The archangel. He wants you to know that he's with you, protecting you. If you think of him, he'll show you a sign, and you'll have comfort in knowing he's with you, wherever you are. There was another spirit guide with him. He looked like an elderly Bantu tribesman, but I have no idea which specific tribe or where he might be from. Nothing to worry about. All you need to know is, your guides are with you."

On my way home, all the traffic lights are green again, but I think nothing of it. As I walk into the house, I notice one of my old cacti I haven't thought about for over a year is in flower. A magnificent white bloom, half the size of the cactus itself, is sticking out of the phallic succulent. It has never flowered before. Ordinarily, I would have documented the full flowering process, but I missed it, and I feel bad for not speaking to my plants in a while. I'm mesmerised by its beauty and stop for a few minutes to touch and take photos of it. I send one picture to Adam, and he replies, "It's beautiful."

Buzzing with spiritual attunement, I can't help but think of my surreal encounter at Michelle's. I ponder what Michelle said after the session then Google "Raphael" and "signs of Raphael's presence". I learn that the archangel shows himself in green colours, and through plants, particularly when they do something unusual. I feel a little wary of delving into things I don't quite understand, so I park my thoughts.

That evening, whilst soaking in an oil-infused bath, the light bulb begins to flicker, a sudden spasm of light, until it eventually blows out, and I see green sparkles of light surrounding me, like a glow of fireflies enveloping my being. To my own surprise, I savour the magical moment as it calms rather than frightens me. Before getting into bed, I go back to look at my cactus and find its flower already closing. I pen a poem before falling asleep.

ONE NIGHT STAND

On the day Raphael visits
they do it well
like a lifetime chance
because they rarely come.

From the depths of
imposing stiffness,
out through the meatus,
white petals break out
to unfurl delicate brilliance
that might never
be seen or felt again—

like the ecstasy
of
a one-night stand.

The day before my flight, I'm packing and repacking my luggage, trying to comply with tight weight restrictions. When I text Adam to tell him I finally resolved to leave my gluten-free bread, Himalayan pink salt and olive oil, he replies with eight laughing emojis.

"My dear Zoro, do you think we have no salt here?"

"I know you do, but this one has a lot more mineral elements… never mind. I must write a poem about packing. Also, I've had to eat your other packet of Percy Pigs I'm afraid!"

"Oh damn, I love those."

"I'll get you some from Duty Free."

"I have suddenly developed a flooding of wanting to be physically with you. Far much stronger than Victoria Falls." Adam sends me a nude. *Damn! This man is as eager as a summer ant,* I titter.

Seeing Adam looking so cheerful in the picture makes me happy, but James is hovering, so I stop texting and put my phone away.

I discreetly kiss Judah goodbye and tell him I might never see him again. I hold him against my chest for a few seconds before returning the fat crystal wand into its velvet pouch and sticking it in one of my old hat boxes in the garage.

I make some popcorn and watch Netflix with Vimbai, John and Peter till the early morning hours. This might be the last time I see my children in a long time. I go to bed without checking my phone, and in the morning, I find a flurry of missed overnight calls from Adam.

"*Iwe dako iwe! Uripiko?* Where the fuck are you?" is the last message he sends.

"My love, I had to watch a movie with the kids last night. Our way of saying goodbye. Anyway, see you soon. I love you. xxx"

On the day of the flight, Adam does not respond to any of my messages, but I now know that's how he operates. He knows my flight details and arrival time and will be waiting for me at O.R. Tambo airport. There's nothing to worry about; he has proven this time and time again.

That afternoon, on the drive to the airport, I rest my eyelids to avoid hollow conversations with James. I quietly celebrate all the times I thought of leaving but failed.

Have you ever sucked your man's dick, knowing fully that only a few hours ago, it was sunk in another hole? Thinking it, smelling it, knowing it, but unable to prove or do anything about it.

All those months spent on Rightmove, scouting for a small flat in faraway places, big enough for just myself and a few belongings. All the dish cloths and kitchen trinkets I bought in Christmas sales for said flat that ended up forgotten behind my folded clothes or inside wedding hat boxes tucked away in my walk-in closet.

Today is a culmination of those seasoned ruminations, once steeped in fear, but now morphed into a sweet reality. Visualising the ragged archipelago of my husband's past puerile behaviour that once obstructed the bigger picture, I applaud myself for finally rising above it and seeing the vista beyond him.

Realising I'm putting my needs first, for once, I suppress a triumphant grin then fall asleep.

At Birmingham airport, after my bags are checked-in, James holds me in a long, tight embrace, then peels himself off to gape into my eyes as if he recognises his younger, restless self in me. He probes for the slightest remnant of loyalty from my eyes that I can feel blinking rapidly. I look away to avoid his eyes that have grown distant with age. He kisses me gently on the lips, then on my forehead.

"I love you Zoro," something he hasn't said in years. "Be safe, ok. Come back to me in one piece." I feel a pang of guilt, and I want to change my mind, but quickly, I push it to the back of my head. I go through airport security and board my flight to Johannesburg.

HIM IN THE FLESH

The ache of desire is not something anyone is meant to get used to.
Having spent so long, too long, typing away the intensity of my heart,
I'm finally confronted with the reality of experiencing him in the flesh.
The avatar in my dreams climbing out of my head to breathe the same air as I do.
To become a reality. To become tangible. To touch him and feel the pulse of his
blood in concert with the palpitations in my chest. I love him.

I love him.

I love him.

Twelve long hours later, my flight lands at O.R Tambo International Airport. After passing through immigration, I nervously wait for my luggage at a carousel, texting messages to James and the children to confirm my safe arrival. I exit the customs area seamlessly and walk into the arrivals' hall, looking out for Adam. I wonder how much shorter or taller he is compared to how he looks in his pictures that always seem to be taken at awkward angles, how he'll smell. I imagine him running out from the waiting crowd, shouting my name, but those are other men running towards their mothers, sisters, wives and girlfriends. *He must be held up in the morning rush or running late,* I think to myself when Adam does not turn up after an hour. Or two. Or five.

Rewinding our conversations, I realise Adam never mentioned he owned a car. There never was a need to. I try to call him, but he doesn't pick up his phone. I send him messages on WhatsApp, Twitter, Instagram, and email. There are no responses.

After a whole day of sitting around and occasionally sprucing up my make-up, I am stale and exhausted. I decide to book myself into a lodge in Sandton on Airbnb and find a taxi outside the airport to take me there. On arrival, I'm given a load shedding schedule by my hosts who explain that depending on what time the electricity goes, they might not be able to turn on their generator.

I'm sure there's a very valid reason why Adam has not shown up. Maybe he's recovering from one of his inopportune splurges. I'll wait for him to get in touch.

After two days of no communication from Adam, I've barely slept or eaten and can feel I'm losing my mind. I try to recite the positive affirmations I could easily sing when I went to therapy, but I can't recall a single word. *Maybe it's because I'm in a foreign place,* I tell myself. I decide to go and find Adam, starting with his address in Yeoville, where I used to send him gifts.

I hire an Uber from Sandton to Yeoville, and a youngish "Zulu" man who speaks English with a Zimbabwean accent comes to pick me up.

As we get closer and closer to Adam's address, I'm shocked by the sharp contrast between the two worlds in Yeoville and Sandton. I notice some seemingly uninhabitable tin shacks, some with two or three storeys and satellite dishes on the roofs. *Poverty drives innovation.* There are mattresses hung outside to dry, poor black people lingering, unbelievable advertisements on posters: "Call this number for an abortion today", "Contact this number for all your *muthi* needs", "Just bring his clothes and Gogo can make you control him". For a second, I think about the tank top I sent to Adam and wonder whether I've been subjected to some kind of spell, but I quickly brush it aside. *No, I just love him.*

The ghetto's commotion is far more amplified than the background noises I often hear through Adam's phone. Taxis play the latest *Amapiano* anthems and some minors in uniform alight to oblige the *Umlando* dance challenge, jiggling their buttocks to phone cameras before jumping onto connecting taxis or disappearing into nearby bottle stores where predators await.

I pause in awe to watch how the dance videos going viral on social media are made, and experiencing the craze in real time feels surreal. I wonder for a moment what sort of homes these children come from. Some of the young girls in short, tight uniforms fraternise with unscrupulous older men, and I'm tempted to drop my own mission to take them home. Then I remember my own vulnerability, and that this is not my war to fight.

Another taxi stops just inches from me, with Shasha's melodious voice painting the atmosphere with memories of home. The voice of Mr Brown singing in chiShona plays next, and I pause for a moment, my heart warming to the thought that I'm not very far from Zimbabwe. The idea to get on a bus and return to my childhood home in Masvingo crosses my mind, but I quickly park it to pursue the critical matter at hand.

Some women hawk and others balance disproportionately large *saga* bags on their heads whilst shushing inconsolable babies on their backs. Cars and jam-packed buses sound their horns intermittently, the discordance amplified by people shouting to each other in foreign languages — it's impossible to tell whether the banter is friendly or hostile. A sharp shrill here, and another one there. A pickpocket whooshes past with chasers closely following behind, and onlookers scream after him. I pick out the words, "*Tsotsi! Tsotsi!*" from their cries.

Remembering the xenophobia attacks I often read about and discuss at length with Adam, I wonder whether the thief might be a fellow Zimbabwean, and I feel exposed. Daunted. Embarrassed.

When we arrive at Adam's address, I stick out like a sore thumb, wearing my stone linen flared pants and a sleeveless woven white cotton top, both by Max Mara, pastel coloured Tory Burch trainers, a navy and white striped Ralph Lauren sun hat, a royal-yellow Prada messenger bag, and like a typical tourist, unable to converse in the local languages. I ask the Uber driver to wait for me, then go to find Adam's place.

There are women and children sitting on the porch of two doors next to each other. The one standing in front of Adam's apartment is heavily pregnant and barely speaks. No one there speaks proper English. I assume the pregnant woman is just a cleaner, or maybe a housemate; after all a bachelor like Adam shouldn't need a whole apartment for himself.

"I am looking for Adam. Do you know him?" The women exhibit blank faces and keep schtum. I find a picture of Adam on my phone and show it to the women. They look at each other first then shake their heads slowly. Although I'm glaringly out of place, the women, who look battered by life, seem unsurprised by my inquisition, or the fact that Adam's picture is on my phone.

I WONDER WHAT HE'S THINKING

Is he happy now that I'm sad?
Is he sad that he does not see me?
Or did he intend to never see me?
Or is he with someone else, watching me?
Without a care in the world how I feel?
Or is he at work pretending to look busy?
Thinking of what he might say to me next?
When he decides to come and find me?

When I find no joy in Yeoville, I ask the Uber driver if he knows how to get to Lephalale from Joburg. "I can help you find transport today *sisi*, and if we find nothing, I can drive you there tomorrow for 5000 Rand."

We leave Yeoville and head for Menlyn Mall, then to Bosman bus terminus, and finally Marabastad taxi rank in Pretoria. No luck. I can smell the crime and poverty in these places, but wanting to spend the rest of my life with Adam outweighs my fears and makes me embrace the diversity in my sight. *These are my African brothers and sisters!*

Nobody knows about "Sprinters" that go to Lephalale, but one of the terminus touts says there is a bus that leaves around 6pm and arrives in Lephalale after 11pm. After a whole day of probing, I phone the hotel I had booked in Lephalale to ask how I might get there, whether there is a hotel shuttle, and how far the place is from where the suggested bus terminates. None of the people at the hotel speak comprehensible English, but I hear "no shuttle".

"Personally, I wouldn't go there *sisi*," the Uber driver volunteers eventually in a piteous voice.

Feeling defeated, I give up on the journey to Lephalale and return to the safety of my Sandton lodge.

ARE YOU SURE YOU WANT TO GO THERE?

where it is blazing hot
and the lovely locals cannot
speak the languages you speak

are you sure
you want to take this bus
that will get you there at night

we phone the lodge
i've booked for my stay
and the voice on the other side says

there are no shuttles
they know not of any taxis &
do not know what we're asking them

so I abort the mission
with my heart in smithereens
gathered neatly, in my hands

While I attempt to puzzle out my next move, the electricity goes, and I can't be bothered to ask anyone to turn on the generator. I unpack and light up some lavender-scented candles I had brought for Adam and watch mosquitoes flying into the Yankee glass jars to be ravaged by the flames. In that moment, as thoughts of Adam torment my mind, I want to be a mosquito. I reach for Adam's whisky and take a hearty swig straight from the bottle. The water of life warms my soul and placates my thumping heart. I remember telling Adam the candles would help him sleep at night and boost his mood when he was feeling low, and he laughed it off. "We don't do scented candles in the ghetto!" I grimace and reach for my journal.

SEETHING IN THE PAINS OF MY OWN DOING

I don't know what to do with the pains inside my bleeding chest—

Must I climb out of my flesh for reprieve?

I stepped out of a dream into a wreckage of a nightmare.

I want my love in Limpopo but how do I get there?

There is no coming back from this.

God—where are you when I need you?

I spend the next seven days unwashed, drinking, waiting, and losing my head.

RUNNER AND CHASER

dear god, we're at it again!

i'm in a dark dingy place

swampy & sweaty & sinking in sludge

ruptured soul, runner & chaser on divergent paths

witnessing a gravitational pull & throbbing—

> *like lachrymose babe detached from mum's raw breast*

> *like warm saline urine trickling over fresh episiotomy*

> *like vicious glochid piercing tender hyponychium*

i'm stuck in black quicksand, pulling me down

& eating me whole & I'm breathing & tasting each grain

of its obscurity as i chew & choke on grit till it oozes out

of my ears & mouth sublimating dark vapour & trying hard

to believe—

> *"we are not our pain*

> *we are not defined by our pain*

> *we are merely observers of our pain"*

i know, i know

but dear god, father dearest—

my mind's ubiquitous like an agitated velociraptor & I can't sleep

it's the pits, my armpits smell like over-spiced stale catarrh, so

pretty please I need the slightest spark to erupt so i can light him up

to singe our souls & be whole again with certainty & truth.

Eventually, I realise that if Adam really wanted to see me, he would have shown up by now. I cannot stand being in Joburg alone, so I contact James, telling him I'm sick and need to come back home immediately. I pack my bags whilst quavering to Simon Chimbetu's *Standby*, my cloud of sadness almost neutralised by a compulsion to laugh at myself for being so dense…

Unoziva chose dhali ndinovimba newe. Moyo wangu bhebhi urere pauri. Dhali, sei kundiita standby? Kundibata senge sipeyawiri. Bhebhi, ini ndave kushandura pfungwa dzanguuuuuu…

I reschedule my flight and give the Airbnb workers all the gifts I'd brought for Adam, then refresh myself with a shower. I chuck £400 worth of the sickening PrEP in the bin. I'm relieved to leave Sandton.

When I arrive at O.R. Tambo, I go through my handbag to inspect the lump sum I brought from the UK; it is not there. *Bomboclaat!* I remember it being in the zipped inner pocket of my messenger bag when I went to Yeoville, but after that hectic afternoon at bus stations in different locations, I didn't think about the money until now. *£30,000!* Bamboozled and deflated, I take deep breaths to avoid collapsing. *All I need is a little alcohol.*

As if the gods have heard my pleas for reprieve, I'm spontaneously upgraded to first class at check-in, and my boarding pass says I'm invited to the Slow Lounge. I'm curious but sceptical, so when I go past airport security, I do some shopping first, using my nearly maxed credit card to buy books by South African women authors, ethnic bead and bone jewellery, and anything that fits in my hand luggage.

I'm excited to see *Mr Loverman* by Bernadine Evaristo and decide to buy it for my dear John. With everything crossed, the payment goes through, but there's nowhere to put the book, and that's my cue to stop. Vimbai will have some of the jewellery and Peter will share biltong and chocolate bonbons with his father. I might get James some Stellenbosch wine onboard. At 2.45 pm I head over to the said "lounge".

On arrival, I ask the white woman at Helpdesk "What happens in a lounge?" Most times I've travelled with James, we've never had the luxury of time to lounge. The woman suppresses a laugh, and in an effort to maintain a straight face, she pulls a condescending one instead and tells me, in a confusing concoction of accents, that there's a free buffet and bar. *Damn! I should have come earlier—free grub must never be refused, especially by the broken-hearted. My flight boards at 3.25pm, so there's little time to do much, but I will do the most.*

The lounge is full of bougie guests who don't fill their plates. I find a vacant table where I dump my bags and fill two plates to the brim, the first with warm jasmine basmati rice and coconut chicken curry and the second with an assortment of cold salads. I go to my table via the bar where I order three large Chardonnays from the bartender who brings the drinks to where I'm seated. The other guests watch me wolfing down platefuls of food in under twenty minutes. I lap the wine at full spate like a parched bitch, then shoot back an unapologetic glare at the observers, thinking to myself, *Adam would have hated it here.*

Later, after take-off, I get up to use the bathroom, and a flight attendant pulls me to the side to tell me I've messed my clothes. *Impossible!* I think to myself but accept the complementary sanitary pads and heated wet wipes. Luckily, I have a spare pair of jogging pants in my hand luggage, which I pull out with fresh underwear, then enter the cramped lavatory. As I wipe off the crimson fluid that's seeped through my beige French knickers to make an unsightly smutch on my cream linen trousers, plum-sized blood clots slide out of my vagina and stick onto the wipes. "Lovely," I mutter under my breath, disgusted by the unseasonable return of my long-forgotten period.

Later, I drown my sorrows in free, expensive gin, snoozing fitfully. The avatar, who I haven't dreamt of since Adam came into my life, returns, holding a gun to its head, and I jump out of sleep as he is pulling the trigger. When my consciousness returns, I can't remember whether the avatar is dead or not. I lapse in and out of sleep, the recurring dream tormenting me until I land in England.

I return from the dead to find my head a sforzando of brass cymbals clashing with relentless drumsticks — the rhythmless din grows louder & louder like a fast approaching stallion, til I feel it swimming in my veins with peptising blood, like sepsis. I need ten triple tots of gin to make me sleep again — a flamboyant flight attendant deflects my rumination to sustenance: "chicken & pasta or ostrich & polenta". Having quit glutenous pasta & red meat, both options make me sick. Plus, dead people need no nutriment & I'm as good as dead. Gluttonous me chooses ostrich & polenta to fill my emptiness. Ostrich meat reminds me of my dead grandmother who used to buy the neck of ostrich when I visited as a kid; I thought it tasted like oxtail, perhaps because it was cut & cooked like it. Either way, it was "a delicacy" so I had to love it despite what I thought. Ah, the good old days when I could indulge with no repercussions. Today — bring on the bloating, inflammation & acid reflux. Fumbling with the food to distract the cacophony within, I cherry pick a cherry tomato garnishing the meal & I hate its taste, or its lack of taste. Whatever happened to sun-kissed tomatoes? Maglia Rosa should be rich & sweet. My mind meanders & I remember his voice notes that used to make me wet…"I want to kisssssss you!" That memory of his hiss makes me spit my tomato with hysterical haste — ah, my tomato! Rich & sweet. I could tell you many stories about "my tomato"…the euphemism for "pussy" coined by women who taught us about periods before we had had our periods…"the tomato is crying" they said we should say when our tomatoes were ripe. Today, I weep with my tomato, crying itself to sleep for the avatar of love who disowned it in a dream. Fuck him! I wipe a tear from my tomato-red eye that I was too shy to look at in the toilet mirror after it shed enough tears to make a Bloody Mary & I'm all but surprised my moist fingers aren't bloody. I pick one slice of ostrich fillet with a steel fork — yes, they have those in business class. Bloody business class! Don't know why they upgraded me to business class when they charged me so much just to get on the flight; flight back to reality from nowhere. He would've had something to say about "the upgrade" & I smile at the thought & I hate myself for thinking of him; I hurt when I think of him. The meat is dead cold & I hate its taste, or it's lack of taste. If I'm going to suffer then it's got to be worth it. I close everything up & push the food away…spot the chocolate mousse on the corner of my tray & I have that instead. It reminds me of him & I hurt & hate myself again! He likes sweet things, like ice cream, jelly babies & me. He calls me "sweetnesssssss" like a sexy serpent; sweet but not sweet, not rich but a runner & obssessor; he's hypnotic; I'm his pet. I chase & chase but can't control him or his mind or my mind when obsessing, yet he can control me, my mind & his mind, he's obsessive — he is there when I don't want him there & I can't push him away & he is not there when I want him there & I can't reel him in — was he ever really there? I know I dreamt him up to escape my grief. Unloved unlovable enamoured. Him. Mirroring. Me. Loving him, like the neck of ostrich while he caused me more grief. Says "I told you I was a fuck-up" to justify himself…paranoid pain-causer causing pain cause he was pain-caused by a pain-causer, what a pain — now I'm paranoid & in pain. I'm fucked up! Tomato weeping…bloating, inflammation & acid reflux… a weeping tomato. The repercussions! I look through the window & watch the clouds dispersing to reveal the truth: beneath me, a serpentine body of water winds like my mind. Oh Limpopo, how badly I yearn to scatter this clatter in your gloom.

WEEPING TOMATO

I return from the dead to find my mind a sforzando of brass cymbals
clashing with relentless drumsticks—the rhythmless din grows louder

& louder... a fast-approaching stallion... 'til I feel it in my veins with
peptising blood, like sepsis. Ten triple tots of gin will push me back into sleep—

a flamboyant flight attendant deflects my rumination to sustenance:
"chicken & pasta or ostrich & polenta?" ...both options make me sick.

Plus, dead people need no nutriment. I remember the good old days when I could
indulge with no repercussions. Bring on the bloating, inflammation & acid reflux!

Fumbling with the food to distract the cacophony within, I cherry pick
a tomato garnishing the meal & I hate its taste, or lack thereof.

Whatever happened to sun-kissed tomatoes? I was his tomato; made me feel like
Maglia Rosa, rich & sweet. My mind meanders & I remember when his simple

words would make me wet... "I want to kiss you!" That memory of his hiss makes me
spit my tomato with hysterical haste— ah, my tomato, juicy & sweet. I could tell

you many stories about "my tomato" ...the euphemism for "pussy" coined
by women who taught us about periods before we first bled...

"the tomato is crying" they said we should say when our tomatoes were ripe.
Today, I weep with my tomato, crying itself to sleep for the avatar of love

who disowned me in a dream. Fuck him! I wipe a tear
from my tomato-red eye that I was too shy to look at in the toilet mirror

after shedding enough tears to make a Bloody Mary & I'm all but surprised
my moist fingers don't come away bloody. I pick one slice of ostrich fillet

with a steel fork—who knew they had proper cutlery on planes. Bloody
business class! I don't know why they upgraded me to business class when

they charged me so much just to get on the flight; flight back to reality
from my business...damn, the busyness! He would've had something to say

about "the upgrade" & I smile at the thought & hate myself for thinking of him;
I hurt when I think of him. The ostrich meat is dead cold &

I hate its taste, or lack thereof. I close everything up &
push the food away...spot the mousse on the corner of my tray &

I eat that instead. Reminds me of him then I hurt & hate! He likes sweet things
like ice cream, jelly beans & my beans. Godlike, amoral, a sexy serpent

who loved to call me sweet; now he's neither here nor sweet
but he runs & obsesses, he's hypnotic. I'm his pet. I sniff & chase

but can't control him or his mind or my mind when obsessing, yet he can
control me, my mind & his mind, he's obsessive—he's there when I don't want

him there & I can't push him away & he's not here when I want him here & I can't
reel him in—was he ever really there? I know...I know... I dreamt him up to escape

my grief. I'm unloved, unlovable, but enamoured. Him. Mirroring. Me.
Loving him while he caused me more grief by justifying the grief

he causes...paranoid pain-causer causing pain because he was pain-caused
by a pain-causer, what a pain, he's a fuck up— I'm fucked!

...bloated, inflamed, with acid reflux... The repercussions! Looking through
the aircraft window I watch the clouds dispersing to reveal the truth:

> *beneath me, a serpentine body of water winds like my mind. Oh Limpopo,*
> *how badly I yearn to scatter this clatter in your gloom.*

When I arrive at Birmingham airport, dejected, I throw myself into James's warm embrace, wishing I'd never left. He holds me for a prolonged period, as if he knows the pain I'm going through. But it's not just pain. There's a twinge of immeasurable guilt too – all the lying and deceit for nearly two years makes me feel foul. I cannot believe I lowered my moral compass to that level, all for a man who was prepared to put my life at risk by luring me to one of the most dangerous places in the world. Despite all this, I find myself missing Adam still. While I now have a deeper appreciation of James's dependability relative to Adam's, a part of me still prefers to sink in the pleasure of lechery.

An hour later, James exits the M5 motorway and cruises into the bucolic Herefordshire countryside via the A449 dual carriageway. His favourite jazz mixtape is on low volume. The guileless charm of Louis Armstrong gravelly crooning *"And I think to myself, what a wonderful world,"* waters my eyes.

James's large, veiny left palm rests on my right thigh, occasionally giving it a gentle squeeze. Using the central armrest to pivot the elbow, my right hand catches my heavy head with a clenched fist. My left hand is buried beneath a caramel cashmere jumper, where my thumb sometimes caresses my underbelly. Comfortable silence prevails between James and me.

I'm acutely aware of the sharp contrast between the freeing dry warmth of the southern hemisphere and the freezing moist cold I have untimely returned to. Despite the heated seats on the highest setting, my muscles constrict to the sudden weather change.

The woe of longing is chewing me inside, and I can feel Adam's energy relentlessly tugging at my blue bean. I know he's thinking of me. Although gravely hung over, I crave a potent drink. I've failed to drink the peppermint and nettle tea James brewed and brought for me in a heated travel mug.

Making a conscious effort to alter my thoughts, I try to remember how I previously managed to quit alcohol. Gritting my teeth and shelving stubborn tears, I turn to my window to seek solace in my unfolding reality. As we pass silhouettes of frosted naked trees, venerable misty streams gurgle beneath a red sky peppered with purple cirrocumulus clouds. A large mystic blue moon reluctantly gives way to the fashionably late golden sun. And I think to myself, *the only thing missing from this masterpiece is green rain. Raphael, are you here?*

I make a mental note to write my inventive thoughts into a poem called 'The here and now', then shift slightly, placing my right hand over James's left that is still on my thigh.

Just then, I spot a murmuration of starlings choreographing a mesmerising aerial display in the sky ahead of us. Their heart-shape formation makes me wish I had the energy to find my phone and take a picture, or open my mouth to say, "Isn't that beautiful?" to James. Instead, I drift into a snooze.

I return to this world when James abruptly removes his hand from my thigh. A stag runs across the driveway and disappears into nearby woodland and James manoeuvres the steering wheel sharply to avoid hitting it. He remotely shuts the high iron gates behind us and says, "Welcome home, sweetie."

TEARS FALLING FROM THE SAME PLACE

In the stillness of my first night back in prison
having escaped to chase after you
before you shot your head dead, the guvnor holds me
tight in his arms like a prodigal pet returned
his heart beating fast with carnal impatience,
mine out-beating his for failed defiance.
He waits for a sign of surrender 'til I gather all my strength
to reconcile my eyes with his & he transforms into you,
love god in my dreams. His hands, his form, his breath, all you.
I search inside my soul for all I'd preserved for you
and my tongue finds itself in a drunken dance with his.

After a few days of feeling sorry for myself, I hoist my hollow self and head for the garden. I try to remember all the things Tim taught me over the last few years on how to gain back control of my life, but I recall none of it. I try to control my breath, but I feel like death. I look around and squirm at how dreadful my garden looks. The space I once designated Mother Nature's playground is now the devil's lair. I'm ashamed to look at my drama of dahlias that seem to facepalm and shake their heads at me in utter disappointment. Most clusters of my plants are already dead and some have been infested with red rust and aphids. My rockeries are colonised by mould and unsightly weeds, which I instinctively pull out each time I walk past.

I drive to the garden centre to buy new plants, then spend hours on end on my knees, playing with dirt outside, like an absentminded child. My tea flask is abundant with gin and cranberry cocktails, providing much needed energy to keep me going. I feel my gut igniting, but the pleasure of intoxication far outweighs the fire burning inside me. I drink frequently to quench my spirit and to numb the throbs of my flesh.

In my earphones, I listen to the playlist Adam created for me, and sometimes random 90s rhythm and blues, abundant with heartbreak anthems.

By chance, James Chimombe plays next. I get up and stagger to a nearby bench to rest and bop my head to *Zvaitika*…

> *Ndaitaura sendine mishonga mukanwa, ukawanza shamwari, uchaaandiramba rimwe zuva. Hona, zvaitika… Ndaitaura sendinopenga, ukawanza shamwari, uchandiramba rimwe zuva. Hona, nhasi, zvaitika…*

Realising my own sinking, I register that I haven't listened to Zim dancehall from the time Adam rubbished it. To find myself again, I tune into a playlist with some of my favourite *mangoma* riddims, *Zimbo*, *Churchyard*, *Panomama munhu*, *Stage*, and I find myself re-energised and outsinging Soul Jah Love on *Mweya Yerima*.

Once more the avatar returns that night, this time in a lucid dream where I'm dressed in military fatigues and my Bad boys combat boots. I've been waiting for him, it seems. He's reciting the poem I love and I'm manoeuvring heavy artillery to aim for his heart.

"You only have to let the soft animal of your body…"

"Oh no you don't!" I pull the trigger of an automatic grenade launcher that devastates Adam's flesh into a million specks of nothing, and the loud bang awakens me to a new triumphant reality. I will never hear from Adam again.

WRITING MURDER

Sleep—
the only place to escape
my heart's ache

Sometimes—
he follows me there
to torment me in my dreams

So—
in my dreams I kill him
to find peace again

The next morning, as I'm driving home from the off-licence, I spot a convoy of black cars behind a hearse and feel water welling up in my eyes. I follow it to the crematorium where black people gather to mourn their loved one. I decide to stay.

I queue up to view the corpse and release the loudest quaking shriek when I see it – the classic, animated Zimbabwean funeral howl is as foreign as my appearance. The elderly woman in the box is not my avatar, but I mourn for her and him. Her own children are kind enough to halt their own tears to console and escort me to my seat where I eventually find my breath.

NO QUESTIONS ASKED

Strangers' funerals
are her pastime of choice,
where she weeps tears of
misadventures unaccounted for.
Somewhere to go when her tear glands need release.
Somewhere to familiarise herself with what's to come,
whilst envying corpses or spirits at last free from flesh.
A party where gatecrashers are
offered hot tea and cakes,
with delicious embraces
—no questions asked.

A couple of weeks later, I receive a message from Adam.

"I think you know what happened. Sleeping with a married woman and accepting her gifts is prostituting myself. As long as we were going to fuck and you were going back to your husband, I was a prostitute. I'm sorry, I had to save both our souls. Everything else, you wouldn't understand. I hope you now know I'm the fuck up that I say I am." I consider not responding, but I'm consumed by a degree of rage beyond anything I've ever felt and can't contain myself.

"So just to prove you're the fuck up you claim to be, you chose to coerce me to come there when you could have told me you changed your mind? I could have saved myself a lot of time and money…I even told you I had changed my mind about coming to see you. Other than the fact that you deliberately wanted to hurt me, I don't think there's anything else to understand. I could have been harmed in Joburg on my own, not knowing where to go, and you were ok with that. After everything we've been through, I don't understand why you chose to do that. Anyway, well done for saving your soul. I hope you remember to throw away everything I've ever given you, including the phone you're looking at right now. Otherwise you'll always be my bitch!"

"It's fine Zoro. I can't say anything more." He screenshots his phone information from the settings page, which reads: Adam's Galaxy A73 5G and proceeds to text, "Thanks for actually reminding me of why I don't want gifts from women. I'm willing to pay back everything you gave me. I'm looking at this phone Zorodzai, you can Google its price in SA. I can't sleep with you for this, then after that you'll go back to your husband. I told you that, but you thought I had a price."

"Adam, are you telling me that every single moment of intimacy we shared over the last couple of years, to you, amounts to prostitution? I was obviously a fool to believe anything you ever said to me. Why would I want to hear more? And to think I was prepared to abandon my whole life in the UK, everything I've ever worked for. For you! Thank you for that profound life lesson." I pause for a bit, trying to figure out what lesson it is I've learnt, then continue, "To think I'd pay for prostitution with sweets and alcohol? You really think I'd pay for your love with those little tokens? I find this insulting honestly!" I'm now panting with fury and despite knowing I need to hold back until I calm down, I send another message, "I gave you everything because I love you. Why can't you see that? I don't need you to pay me back."

"I never asked you to come here, Zorodzai. Check your messages and you'll see that I said it was ok for you to not come, but then you insisted you wanted to. I insisted it was not morally right to sleep with another man's wife, but you said we had to sleep together. I've told you many times, if you can't leave your marriage, it means you're okay where you are. I have the utmost respect for women, and one day you'll thank me for what I did." I want to ask him what drugs he's on because this doesn't sound like the man I fell in love with.

"Stop gaslighting me, Adam! Your sudden moral high ground is shocking. Did you not know I was married when you were sending me nudes just the other week? And the week before that? And the one before that? What were you hoping to achieve by sending me those pictures? You know you were breadcrumbing me. Whenever I sounded like I was losing interest in you, you'd drop me more crumbs. Stop bullshitting. I ain't got time for this! *Uri mbgwa yemunhu!*"

I go back to try and reread our old messages, just in case I misunderstood him, but realise before I go too far, that this mind game is no longer worth playing. I decide to block Adam on all communication channels and a gentle wadding immediately begins to fill up the cracks of my broken heart.

I DON'T SPEAK ROTTWEILER

He's told me before
that he's a fuck up
but I couldn't comprehend it—
I don't speak Rottweiler.

My heart risen from the dead
wanted only one thing—
to live again, fully, with a pet this time
but he said, no thank you to picket fences.

Even an animal tamed
is prone to attacking its owner;
we've all heard of what these pets can do, but
a woman in love can't comprehend all that.

When I sensed the looming offence
in his words said & unsaid, violence
encrusted with golden breadcrumbs
I devoured dubiety & cursed my gut.

My heart is dead again—
he fucked it up real good this time &
watched me squirm beneath his paws
as I choked on his crumbs of love.

He's dead now, I had to kill him
and he haunts me in my dreams
barking, 'I told you I was a fuck up!'
—I don't speak Rottweiler.

Two days after blocking Adam, I feel an energy coiling around my heart like a python constricting its prey and at once, I know. When I go online, I find Adam following me on all social media platforms with a new account. The name on the handle is not Adam's and he changes it frequently. In the profile picture, Adam is with a woman hugging him affectionately from behind. They're posing in front of a Christmas tree. *Yet this motherfucker said he didn't believe in celebrating commercialised religious holidays – Christmas was the white man's cretinous holiday hinged on capitalism, and Jesus wasn't even born in December, he said!*

The other woman looks hauntingly familiar but because she's not facing the camera, it takes me a while to figure out who she is. After hours of pondering, I finally remember – it is the woman I saw at Adam's door in Yeoville. *What. The. Fuck?* I immediately feel an expansive repulsion towards Adam. *Why could he not be honest with me about this woman as I was honest with him about James? How many times did I ask him whether he had moved on? Could she have been in his life all along? And why is he rubbing this in my face?*

I try to imagine Adam sleeping with the pregnant woman, the way he said he would worship my vagina, which he called "his pussy". Replacing myself with the pregnant woman in the dreams I've harboured for two years paints Adam the devil incarnate.

LET'S TAKE A FAG BREAK

I want to flush the little shit down the toilet drain and drown it to its death so its wish can come true. So it can stop burning whatever touches it, like an electric catfish. Social media catfish selling dreams of lush love, misrepresenting love til it burns out to reveal the truth, but never refunding the missold dreams! My pain stories sell well to shits like him; the hard type that brings immediate relief to your gut once it's out of your system – now floater staring at you before the final flush. I stare back and ask it why I found solace in shit. It opens its mouth and says shit is the place people like me drown their sorrows by allowing themselves to be sucked in til they too turn into shit... my heart is tired of think pieces with no nuance, and needs to stop for a fag. Come and smoke with me...

STOP FOR A FAG

I want to flush the little shit down the toilet drain
and drown it so its wishes can come true.
To stop it burning whatever touches it like an electric catfish...
Social media catfish selling dreams of lush love, misrepresenting
'til it burns out to reveal the truth, with no refund for missold hope.
My pain story sells well to shits like him; the hard type that brings
relief to your gut once it's out of your system–
now a floater staring at me before the final flush.
I stare back and ask why I found solace in it & it replies:
> *'Shit is where people like you drown their sorrows*
> *Allowing yourself to be sucked in til you too turn into shit...*
> *I am you and you are me— you're looking at you!'*
My heart is tired of think pieces with no nuance
and needs to stop for a fag.

At this point, it is not the mistimed discard by Adam that stings me the most, but the man's steadfastness in premeditated depravity and his nonchalant administration of more pain where it's already overflowing. It's his entitlement to women's time and their hearts that pulls my last straw.

Nauseated by the situation, I reach for a bottle of vodka to ease my grief. I have become desensitised to the alcohol-induced fireworks causing a raucous in my stomach.

STINKING REALISATION

I imagined your lips
macadamia-flavoured, 'til
your mask dropped to reveal the
bastard who ripped my heart to shreds
(and now) I know
you taste like forty-year-old eggs
pickled in spit & piss in an old glass jar
on a shelf behind the bar
of a squalid english pub
enticing the nescient bird.

Sometimes I wonder if Adam simply asked his housemate to pose with him in the pictures to make me jealous, but a few weeks later, Adam posts photos of his new-born baby on the social media handle that nobody follows. The baby looks just like him. He uses his usual account that I blocked, to like and comment on his own posts.

Poor child! And its love-deprived mother, clueless of the vileness in store for her. For a songbird never alters its birdsong. All that time Adam spent talking to me, where was she? Did he have any love left for her after pouring so much into my empty cup?

I can't help but marvel at the enigma that is Adam. I've decided to ignore his drama to focus on healing my broken heart. But try as I might to dismantle the energetic consonance between us, it remains.

Now perpetually inebriated, I contemplate finding something stronger to dull my torment. The tomato weeps still, as does the prismatic eye of my I.

THEY DON'T EXIST

The one I fell in love with
was mirroring me the whole time
'til he got tired of the obsessing act
and all became clear—
he doesn't exist & all this time
I've been loving myself

With my dreams jet-washed into oblivion, I make a greater effort to get over what happened. I eventually resolve that my pain is not a result of what Adam did to me, but that I allowed it to happen, just like I allowed James to hurt me all those years ago. *I'm not made for this world...I hate it here... I don't belong here! Perhaps Adam's love was just a figment of my imagination.*

I feel an enormous part of myself dying at this realisation. My ego has been cruelly injured, but I begin to find the pain gratifying. I will not take for granted how beautiful it has been, to feel again. These new feelings, steeped with stale love, make me experience a strange sensation – I seem to enjoy the agony in my heart.

"You've lost a lot of weight honey," James seems concerned.

"Is that not what you've always wanted? A thin wife."

"You don't look well, Zoro. Take it easy with the bottle."

"Kiss my black ass."

PAYDAY SALAD

The only way

to get over my heartache

is to indulge in it, savour it

like a payday salad with all the bits & frills—

craisins, almonds, feta

pomegranate & sunflower seeds

'til it becomes ordinary, boring, forgettable

like I am to him

What goes up must come down. My pendulum of emotions swung high to the left where I experienced a type of joy and freedom I had never felt before. I don't care whether it was real or not. What matters is I felt it. And now, the pendulum has swung to the right, as it must, and I am dealing with the emotions there.

All those things I read about twin flames when I was blinded by passion suddenly make sense. "Both people lack the skills, capacity and discipline to have a workable relationship in this lifetime, so the relationship cannot work in the long-term... Without this experience, we will not be forced into rebuilding ourselves mindfully in preparation for our life partner. This relationship highlights what we can't live with and what we can't live without."

One morning, feeling a little optimistic about life, I reach for my Tibetan singing bowl. It usually hums ancient echoes, its resonant tones dissolving the tension in my flesh until I find solace. Today, the brass bowl sounds more or less like a heifer giving birth, its dissonance mirroring my own meaningless life. In a desperate bid to find mind and body balance, I attempt 3 sun salutations before flumping into savasana in resignation, and I feel at peace in the corpse position. In the spirit of staying positive, I think, *now that Adam is gone, I might just give James and I another go, despite my intuition screaming "No!"*

Being who I am, I saunter up to our office to do something I've not done in years. I sit behind his desk, guessing his password until the two of us looking happy in The Maldives marvellously disappear to reveal numerous open pages. Ah-ha! The euphoria of success never gets old. Now, where to start…

On James's internet browser, at least twenty tabs are open, and I start going through each one of them to see what he's been up to. First his golf schedule, then Gmail, and Yahoo. *I'll skip these for now.* On the forth tab is a money transfer website where James is already logged into. *I'll come back to this!*

On the fifth tab, I find a mirror of my phone, with all conversations between Adam and me on all my social media platforms in plain sight. Our exchanged images are squarely arranged in a grid on one side of the screen, some of them favourited. The shame of seeing my naked body on James's computer is confounding. Even Adam's nakedness that I once slavered over is now distasteful. Mortifying! My heart races out of control, its forceful pounding echoing throughout my body. I immediately sober up.

James drives in and parks outside. The sound of his car is unusually amplified. On the next tab, I see images from the garage, the garden, and every room in the house. When I click each room, I can hear everything going on in it. I find the office screen and look up to spot a fat spider stuck to the ceiling. I wave at it and see myself on the screen. *Hidden cameras? What the fuck, James!*

James enters the house, calmly calling my name, but his footsteps towards me sound rather urgent. My stomach churns with dread. I pull the plug out of the socket to switch off his computer and replace it with the vacuum cleaner. I fly out through the French doors, past the potted Xanadu and the Monstera whose leaves I break. I brush against the bird bath and graze my right ankle, going off balance to land on my face within a newly planted hedgerow of mature hydrangea shrubs. A zephyr of long-tailed tits bursts out of the bushes, their chirps of panic echoing through the crisp air. "Sorry!" I mouth to the birds and to my poor plants, then station there until the coast is clear. I taste fresh blood. *My tongue!* My whole body is inflamed. My mind, demented with confusion, is like seed scattered on barren land.

***

Exhausted from playing the game of life, I truly believe that only in death will I achieve equilibrium.

GOING HOME

My world stands still, hardens
to the dropping Celsius and cracks open
before crumbling into a heap of dust
like a new grave without the
stone and concrete, no epitaphs yet,
oozing truth like my love for the man I never met.
He is not here, but he is there; that's neither here nor there—
at the realisation that my dream has been just that
I'm trying to process how love so vast could be defeated so fast

but the answers come naught, and
a heap of dust calls me back home

That evening, after serving James and Peter burnt cottage pie, the full moon lures me back into the garden where I sit beneath an indigo sky, sipping a concoction of the finest spirits.

My body temperature rises, and I slide off the wooden banana bench as if the earth is pulling me in. I drop into the dew-soused carpet of early wild-flowers with a gentle thud, like a ripe tomato tired of waiting to be plucked off the vine. Lying on my back, I lengthen, then spread into a T position, ready to make snow angels, except there is no snow, and my life force is subsiding.

Savouring the cool bliss rising from my feet, spreading upwards to commune with the heat in my chest, I try to count the stars in the ether – three, ten, hundred, then a myriad, and the world begins to spin unceremoniously like the worst case of vertigo. I tense my body briefly then, remembering to control my breath. I relax and release a long exhale.

I can hear James's faint call in the distance, then sirens moments later, but I only drift further away, faster. Like a speck of dust in an industrial machine, I whirl in a tunnel with a light glimmering at the end of it. The velocity of brightness is amplified with each spin as I travel to merge with the dazzling light.

Part two

The return of Mudavose

The spirit rises like temperate mist, hailing its newfound uninhibition, having unrobed itself of throbbing flesh. Its aura amalgamates into a pastel ball of light gliding towards a higher consciousness, but to the human eye gazing, it is only a luminous star shooting in the sky. At a cave-like opening, three spirits wait to usher through the neophyte. A velocity of brightness hails the incoming resident who merges with its brilliance and immediately becomes love.

"Welcome home, Zorodzai!"

"Hello…I mean thank you. Where am I? What is happening?"

"You are home!"

"Home?"

"Yes, home. To use an expression from the physical realm, you have died. Welcome to Nyikadzimu."

"Oh! I feel free… and full of joy!"

"As you should, Zorodzai."

"There is so much love here…"

"Thank you for agreeing to switch. I must not waste too much time here as your flesh awaits my spirit. If I'm late, the humans might dispose of your body before my arrival." The four spirits look down in that moment to witness a woman's body being collected from a garden on a stretcher bed. It is pushed into the back of an ambulance and rushed to a local A&E, medics frantically bidding to resuscitate it. When the spirit sees James, who was its husband, and three children in distress, it wonders, *will they cope without me?*

"They'll be fine. When I walk into your body, they'll think you're still with them, and I will do my best to be gentle."

"Wait, you know what I'm thinking?"

"In this realm of consciousness, we can converse by thought and discern the truth that way."

"Who are you? And why are you going back there?"

"My name is Mudavose. That is the last name I was given by my great grandfather in a previous lifetime, for I am the one who loves all. I'm the prophecy of Chaminuka, that to love one another is the only way to heal the damage of subjugation caused by the wreckage of colonisation. Our people have suffered enough. The children of the soil are sick. They are scattered all over the world like sunflower pollen blown by the wind, until they are diluted and forgetful of who they are and where they're from. *Vana vevhu!* They have become prisoners of their own minds. Their minds go with the wind, floating aimlessly like Baby's Breath in far flung places. They seek solace in all the wrong places, trying this and that in order to find themselves. They are in pursuit of non-existent greener pastures, trying to find *chokubata* in other lands where they are seen as shrapnel. And the children, as a result, treat one another like detritus. Takers elevate themselves by demeaning *vana vevhu* then shake their heads in pompous pity before proceeding to enslave them and bruising the children's egos beyond measure. They do not understand who these children are. Children of the soil of a place where civilisation was born. The Great Dzimbabgwe.

Yet my people are naked and hungry. There's fear and agitation. There's no hope. The sound of their cries can no longer carry on, flouted. I hear my people calling. I hear the *nhare* calling in the ancestral realm. My people will be rescued from this state of turmoil. The *bira* is relentless in its call for help. I hear the vibrations of the *mbira*, the thunderous *ngoma* in concert with meditative claps of tough, dry hands, the whispers of rattling *hosho* transacting with the bellowing *bhosvo*, and the rhythmic thud of *mbakumba*-dancing feet. They have awakened us. We have heard the call."

"And why have you chosen my body?"

"I've been roaming *nyikadzimu* for a timeless period, and I've been assigned this special task by Mwari. I'm a member of your spirit clan, and I've chosen you as a means to return to earth to construct the vessel of Mwari's voice, so that it may breathe life into her people again. I am to take the vessel to a place where it will be safely guarded by *mhondoro* until the end of time. And love will be restored in the hearts of the children of the soil. All turmoil will at once be gone. And Mwari's people will know peace again."

"How on Earth will you do that?"

"I have the experience. In my previous incarnations, I journeyed with the Lemba who carried the *ngoma lungundu* on their migration down South from the lost city of Sena in Yemen, via the Abyssinian Sea, into Guruuswa in Tanganyika, then to Mapungubgwe in Limpopo. We married Bantu women along the way, and in Mapungubgwe, we built the first houses of stone. There, the *ngoma lungundu* was stolen from us by the Nguni, and it exploded due to misuse. It had been handled by adulterated hands who sought only the powers of the *ngoma*, and not what it represented."

"I've heard of that drum. Is it the one that used to be beaten once by the Lemba to destroy whole armies during battle? The one subject to never-ending human debate on whether it was Moses's ark of the covenant?"

"That's the one! Its acacia pieces were scattered and stored in various places after the explosion. We migrated north again, to escape the calamities that befell us after the demise of the *ngoma lungundu*. On our way to Dzimbabgwe, we stationed in places where we designated names reminiscent of the holy drum."

"No way! Which ones?"

"Ngundu – the drumbeat onomatopoeia, and Ngomahuru – the large drum, to name but a few."

"I see."

"My mission requires me to return to the physical realm. This time, not via the tunnel of birth through a woman's womb, but through a switch with your soul."

"You do realise you're going to be in the body of a woman, don't you?"

"Ah, yes. I've not been a woman before, which is why it is of paramount importance to evade childhood conditioning that comes with being born a baby…that would hinder the sacred mission. *Mwari* will guide me."

"So, out of our whole spirit clan…you still haven't explained why you chose me."

"Women's bodies are the only portals to earth, but there are two other reasons. Women are historically the makers of sacred drums. Traditionally, only *makhadzi* are worthy to create them, and only their hands are intended to beat these vessels through which the voice of *Mwari* can be heard. Women are emblems of life, you see. The second reason is equally critical. You had become a mere mindless automaton, with no more will to live. And many lifetimes ago, you agreed to exchange your body for my fleshless bliss, when the time came."

"Why didn't I die sooner?"

"You could have. You were so spiritually attuned, we felt all your calls and sent help, but you evaded the opportunities we sent. Eventually, the universe sent your mirror soul to love and break you. On your fruitless quest for love in South Africa, your tour guide would have taken you to Mapungubgwe as arranged, and he would have robbed and stabbed you there. Our switch would have happened during your coma in the ICU. Then the dubious pills you bought online. One more week of those on your overworked liver would have killed you, but you stopped the poisoning because you couldn't handle the side-effects of the medicine. When that didn't work out, we sent you cancer."

"Cancer?"

"Yes, why else would a menopausal woman start bleeding suddenly? Sooner or later, you would have been diagnosed with stage four cervical cancer. You would have been offered a hysterectomy, and our switch would have taken place during your surgery. Anyway, the drinking worked, and alcohol poisoned you. Your twin flame drove you there and accomplished his mission after all."

"What can I say? Thank you for rescuing me. I'm sorry I made you wait for so long!"

"Don't apologise, this realm of consciousness is timeless. What may have been years on earth could be a second or millennium. Time – a human construct, is meaningless here."

"So, what happens now?"

"You shall be shown your Akashic records, before returning to Earth for another adventure, to learn the lessons you failed to learn. Until we meet again, goodbye." Without waiting for a response, Mudavose's essence enters the cave-like opening and glides down to the physical realm, a dark veil of ignorance progressively swathing the spirit, until it enters the human body through the medulla oblongata at the base of the brain. The body makes a jerking movement, and the flesh of Zoro is confirmed alive by the medics who have been resuscitating it.

In *nyikadzimu*, the presence of Mwari is palpable and the spirits have 360 degrees peripheral vision. A large screen appears before the three souls, airing Zoro's previous lifetimes in their minutest detail, including when it committed suicides and was returned to the school of Earth. How the spirit was at one point James's mother who died giving birth to him. How the spirit split into two during another lifetime, one of which is currently incarnated as Adam. Future lifetimes are revealed, where the halved spirit unites and all its life lessons are eventually learned, thereafter elevating it to an enlightened spirit, like Mudavose. It is at this point that Zoro realises her life on Earth was all an illusion.

Back on earth, coming to terms with the reality of human embodiment in a body teeming with illusion, delusion, error, pain and hopelessness, the spirit of Mudavose grieves whilst tussling for freedom. It travels to the base of the spine in pursuit of the slightest smidgen of positive energy, but finds only stagnancy and climbs back up in pursuit of respite to find the portal impassable. The flesh squirms like a worm probed by a curious child.

Stuck in Zorodzai's body, the spirit lapses into agonal dirge, *why oh why?* And the voice of *Mwari* responds:

The body's circadian rhythm is categorically tangled. The being enters its native state, becomes unconscious, and the medical team confirms, "She's in a coma".

***

Vimbai softly rubs her mother's feet, absent-minded, unexpectant, a weekly ritual that has become the zenith of her existence. She takes Wednesdays off to go and sit at the bottom end of a bed in room 18 in the neuro recovery wing at St. Ethelwald's private hospital, waiting for her mother's return. She's entranced by the essences of jasmine and sandalwood wafting across the air, schmoozing but anticipating naught.

"Mum. Today feels like a good day for you to wake up." Her outbreath spells a longing she cannot quite articulate. A slight increase in the pressure of her knead speaks of her desperation for maternal affection. "I've always thought you had nice legs, mummy. Dad is a lucky guy. He misses you…and the boys. But I think I miss you more than anyone else. It's hard being the only girl in that house you know…"

"I can only imagine, sweetie." Mudavose, now Zoro wiggles their big toe to confirm the return of life force to their body. As if she has encountered a ghost, Vimbai abruptly drops her mother's foot and runs out of the room, screaming. A few minutes later, a team of medics surround the patient's bed.

"It doesn't feel like her, daddy." Vimbai tries to explain to James.

"Don't worry *nana*, it'll take a while for her to come round."

"She's never called me sweetie before. And she sounds different!"

"She's been in a coma for a year, so she'll have severe post-traumatic amnesia. It'll take a while for her to be as you remember her," says one of the doctors in the room.

"I'm fine. I want to go home," their voice is hoarse and poised.

"Really honey? I think they'll need to keep you in for a few more…"

"No. I want to see the boys!"

"The boys are on their way." James holds Zoro's hands to calm her down. When the boys arrive, Zoro doesn't remember their sons' names, but wastes no time getting to know them again.

"So, you. With the cheerful jacket on. What have you been up to?"

"Um mum, it's me, John. Tarquin and I have just come back from a few weeks of travelling. It's really lovely to have you back, mummy." Their face is blank - no idea who Tarquin is.

"And I'm at uni now, mum. It's Peter."

"Ah, my lovely boys. You've grown into real beauties. I'm planning a little adventure in Dzimbabgwe. Maybe we could all go!"

"Where?" They all exclaim in unison, exchanging glances. The entire medical team is shocked by how vibrant Zorodzai appears. Whereas they expect them to be in a vegetative state, they sit up initially, and by the next morning, they're taking long walks around the lush hospital gardens, insisting they cannot be confined to a tiny hospital room riddled with stagnancy when there's so much goodness to be taken from nature.

When Mudavose is released from hospital, they experience relentless dreams about going back home to complete their mission. They don't recall what the mission is, but know they must go, and further instructions will be revealed when they arrive. Three days after returning to consciousness, they waste no time telling James that they need to go home.

"I need to be in Dzimbabgwe my love. Only the sun there, and the herbs growing in the rich red soils beneath it can heal me."

"Why do you keep calling it Dzimbabgwe?"

"Because that is what it is called. That is where I come from. The stone houses of Mwene Mutapa are many. Everyone knows that!"

"It's Zimbabwe, love."

"No. Zimbabwe means one big house of stone, which is not true of my birthplace. Those who came to steal our land and lumped all the tribes of Mwene Mutapa into one, fortified their lies by giving our land a name that implies our country is one big stone house, with one silly language they called Shona. What is Shona? Mscheeew!" They roll their eyes, appalled.

"Are you ok, honey?"

"Yes, James. I am a Ka-RA-nga from Dzimbabgwe, child of Ra the sun god. And I'm going back home to heal my people."

"Who are your people?"

"The Bantu, of course!"

"Haah? Your head's clearly not ok. *You* need to heal, darling. Who will look after you there?"

"Ha! Don't you mean who will look after *you* here? I'll be fine. I'll go to my father in Masvingo if I need help."

"Your father is old, Zoro. The guy is in his 80s, remember?"

"What's that got to do with anything? A body can do whatever it likes if the spirit is willing."

"But I've missed you, Zoro. I need you here with me."

"No, you don't. You were fine without me for a year. You'll be ok." James is more surprised by Zoro's perceptiveness than their coldness. He had hoped a break from reality would bring them back rearing into their domesticated self.

"What about our children?"

"Children? Are you kidding me? These guys are old enough to look after themselves!"

"Do you still love me?"

"Yes. More than you will ever know, but without attachment, the possessiveness or co-dependency that consumed us in the past. I also love myself and everyone on earth. I can't do that properly if I'm here channelling all I've got into one person." Realising that James doesn't understand them, they smile and add, "You can come and join me in Dzimbabgwe if you really want to be with me. I don't belong here." The conversation ends there, and the matter is not brought up again.

A week later, they arrive at RG Mugabe International Airport where a taxi driver awaits in the arrivals' hall, an A4 placard with the name 'Mudavose' covering his chest. Their razor-sharp intuition informs them the driver is a spirit guide.

"*Kwazuvai. Ndini* Mudavose."

"I've been instructed to take you to Domboshava, where your guide awaits. Here, take this." The driver hands Mudavose some herbs and a large *nhekwe* of *bute rehondo*, which they gracefully accept.

"Thank you. What shall I do with these?"

"Take a pinch of herbs from each packet, mix them in your palm then eat them immediately. You are not allowed to spit them out. When you're done, pour a little *bute* from the *nhekwe* container onto your palm. Pinch a little and sniff it hard."

"But I don't smoke…"

"Who said anything about smoking? This is not tobacco. It's a concoction of *chambgwa, muhacha, mupfura,* and other special ingredients I won't get into now. *Bute* is our sage. It wards off evil spirits and bad energies whilst connecting you to Mwari via our ancestors. You need to take it. And remember to spill a little oblation on the ground for the ancestors and ask them for their guidance." As Mudavose chews the bitter herbs, their face frowns but their body straightaway strengthens. They pinch some *bute* powder from the centre of their cupped left palm and sniff it through their right nostril, then the left. The earthy smell fills the vehicle. It rushes to their brain like a small swarm of happy bees, and they follow it there and back.

There is a mighty sneeze thereafter! And another. And another. Dark mucus suddenly gathers and descends their nostrils. They desperately pull it back in as they swiftly retrieve pocket tissue. After clearing their nasal clogging, they sniff the *bute* again. Some of it goes to their head once more while some of it side-tracks down their gullet. In no time, they learn to channel it where it needs to be, sometimes the head, sometimes the stomach. Either way, the *delicious* gift is not to be wasted.

"You're a fast learner," the driver peers through the rear-view mirror and smiles.

For the first time since returning to flesh, Mudavose remembers who they are, like dissipating mist. Now a lot more aligned spiritually with Mwari, their mission becomes clear.

"It feels like this has been a missing piece to my puzzle. Thank you."

The driver nods in response, then speaks after a few moments of thought. "Domboshava is the hill of *vaera shava*. As you know, the prophecy you're about to fulfil was made by Chaminuka, a *mhondoro* who advocated for a peaceful co-existence amongst the children of the soil. He was of the Shava Mazarura totem clan. So, it is only right that your feet step on the soil of Domboshava to announce your arrival and mark the beginning of this critical journey. From there, you will be guided to your people - the water spirits." He turns the volume up, and the radio begins to play a local arts group venerating the high spirit in a *Mhande* song:

> *Chaminuka ndimambo*
> *Ahe ndimambo*
> *Ahe ndimambo*
> *Shumba inogara yoga musango*

It is early evening when Mudavose is dropped off near the back access to the ruddy-ridden boulders of Domboshava. The taxi driver instructs her to climb to the summit of the hill, where the guide will meet her. As soon as Mudavose reaches the top, she sprinkles *bute rehondo* to the east, west, north, and south, announcing her arrival to *makombgwe enyika* and venerating Chaminuka and his lineage. As they sniff more *bute*, they feel lighter and lighter, like a bird of prey about to take flight.

In no time, *chamupupuri* appears in the horizon, and Mudavose can hear the children herding cattle nearby lapsing into song and coiling their waists to mimic the phenomenon fervently dancing towards them.

> *Chamupupuri chauya*
> *Chamupupuri icho*
> *Chamupupuri chainda*
> *Chamupupuri ze-eeeeee!*

> *Hecho chauya!*
> *Hecho chainda!*
> *Hecho ze-eèeeee!*

The whirlwind approaches gradually until it engulfs and whisks Mudavose off the ground. In the eye of the whirlwind is a serene lake, Dzivaguru. A magnificent creature emerges from the centre of the crystal-clear body of water. It has a human upper body, with soil-coloured hair bunched into long strands of *mhotsi*. Its lower body resembles a luminous fish.

"*Mhoro* Mudavose. Welcome to Mugomba! I am your guide, Dananai," it says, waving, and Mudavose notices the fins under its arms and on its back, and webs between the fingers.

"*Kwazuvai* Dananai. I'm pleased to meet you." Mudavose is mesmerised but not surprised.

"KaNgoma - you are a deity who chose to incarnate for a divine mission. I've been sent by Mwari to help you construct the vessel of his voice – Ngoma Inoti Ngundu. You will carve the drum from a branch of the ancient *muchechete* trees flanking the Conical Tower at Great Zimbabwe. The wood must be cured for 108 days in the sacred waters of Dzivaguru to fortify it. The drum hide will be skinned from an animal species unknown to humans, one that only I have the strength to catch, here in Dzivaguru. That skin holds powers to repel prying humans. Once you complete this task, I'll take you and Ngoma Inoti Ngundu to Mabgweadziva, where Mwari will tell us where to retain the vessel of his voice. Thereafter, you will remain custodian of the sacred drum until the end of your time."

"I understand."

Dananai beckons Mudavose, and the fins on her back transform into majestic wings that transport them to their destination.

A few months later, on a mild morning, Mudavose latches onto Dananai's muscular back, and they glide in the gentle *Nyamavhuvhu* breeze towards Mabgweadziva, the intricately carved Ngoma Inoti Ngundu floating above them. The patterns engraved on it reflect the wondrous flora and fauna of Mugomba.

Rainmakers from all Bantu tribes have been summoned in a shared dream, to travel to their spiritual headquarters where Mwari's voice will speak to them for the first time in a long time. Thousands of Bantu pilgrims arrive, clapping their hands and bowing their heads to announce their arrival to the custodians of Matonjeni, *vaera shoko*. To show reverence and humility, the pilgrims remove their shoes at the three entrances of the sacred shrine, a serene cave beneath the overhanging granite boulders at the hills of Matobo. The soil scent of *bute* passing from palm to palm ignites the atmosphere.

Without stopping to rest or eat, they stomp their bare feet to the triple metre of *Mhande* rhythm and *makwa* handclapping as Mudavose beats Ngoma Inoti Ngundu insistently, its sound reverberating within the granite walls of the shrine.

Ngu-ndu! Ngu-ndu Ngu-ndu! Ngu-ndu- ngu!
Kwazivai Tovera, mudzimu dzoka!
Haiwaiwa hoyiye, mudzimu dzoka!
Vana vanogwara, mudzimu dzoka!
Kwazuvai Tovera, mudzimu dzoka!
Ngu-ndu! Ngu-ndu Ngu-ndu! Ngu-ndu- ngu!

Mbira maestros vigorously thumb the *nhare*, telephoning *vadzimu* for their help to call on Mwari's voice. Frisson and horripilation engulf the crowd as *doro rechiKaranga* is passed around in specially made earthenware pots, and they begin to hear The Voice.

Children of the soil, I have not forsaken you. I never stopped speaking, but you could not hear my voice, because this shrine was contaminated by those who left their own lands to come here and take what was not intended for them. They took what was yours, disturbed your peace, gave you names you could not pronounce and foods you could not digest, until you forgot who you were. These destructive forces dragged you down, and your world sunk into a darkness deeper than any other. You can hear my voice now, and you will rise towards the light and be restored. I am the light. I am love. You will feel my love, then one another's, and when your bodies remember what love is, you will heal and begin to see yourself in a positive light.

A new, unadulterated vessel of my voice has been carved, and you have gathered here to celebrate it. Through Ngoma Inoti Ngundu, I will speak to you, and your lives will be repaired. This ngoma will be installed at the top of the Conical tower – the epicentre of your cultural heritage, the fortress of your country. It will stay there for all to see and hear my voice.

You must live by hunhu principles, so that when you transcend to higher realms of existence, you become not just an ancestor, but mudzimu. You must honour vadzimu, the authors of your heritage who speak to me on your behalf. That will awaken mhondoro to take possession of The Great Enclosure at Dzimbabgwe until the end of time, and Ngoma Inoti Ngundu will neither be stolen nor silenced again.

Earlier ngomas buried in the hearts of mountain caves perished and your sickness worsened. The last authentic ngoma was taken from Dumbghe, the eastern facing rock that bows to the rising sun to manifest renewal and innocence. From there, it was stored in Harare museum where it was taken by your own brothers who thought the ngoma would keep them alive to rule forever. It was deleterious of them to think I am for a single person, tribe, or nation. Learn from their deaths that nobody can keep my voice for themselves! Cease and desist the culture of individualism that rubbed onto you from the takers!

When Ngoma Inoti Ngundu takes its designated position, all deadly diseases will disappear. Poverty, hunger, corruption, conflict, disease of your minds and all ills of this land will be cured. You have toiled like slaves on your own fertile soil, rich with gleaming stones that only benefit a few who rob their own. Remember, you are descendants of a civilisation that was sophisticated enough to build a vast city with dry stone walls with no mortar or cement. Never forget who you are and where you're from. So, go forth and tell every child of this soil scattered across earth:

You are elevated from NO-body to SOME-body!
Arise, child of the soil, arise! Rise towards the light!
You are NOT a victim of 3-dimensional people!
You are love! You are victorious!

A temperate torrent descends from the bright cloudless sky and the pilgrims savour the opulence of petrichor, feet stomping, bodies swaying to the sound of *Ngoma Inoti Ngundu.*

"Look! *Murarabungu!*" A pilgrim points to a tertiary rainbow each with supernumerary bows, arching across the sky. Dazed by the phenomenon, the dancing rainmakers, now in a trance, graduate their singing to scats of melodious syllables.

> *Aho hendeya ndeya ho*
> *hore herey yey yey*
> *woyihe hiye hiye hiye hiyerere*

In that moment of spiritual ecstasy, twelve fish eagles hover over the crowd in formation and call nine times to Dananai and Mudavose as they lead the way to Dzimbabgwe.

Epilogue

After one month with Dananai, you exit a whirlwind and stroll up to the lifeguards at the Mutirikwi shores. "Please, take me to Garisanai. And tell my people that I shall catch the crocodile tonight!" Immediately, a mist engulfs the landscape, and the people of Dzimbabgwe know, *zvine chirevo*.

Garisanai is pleased to see you back in good shape. She ushers you to your new chambers within the fortress. When she leaves you there to rest, you shut your eyes and find yourself within the network of tunnels beneath the hills of Dzimbabgwe. The place is mystically tranquil, and as you explore the space, you hear voices behind you, "Murenga! Murenga!"

You look behind but can't see anyone.

"Down here!"

You look down and see them. Two zebra-shaped clay pots. You think hard about where you've heard of talking pottery, and they tell you.

"It's us, Pfuko yaKuvanji. You need to wake up and prepare for battle! Zhingoz are coming for you! Call for us on the battlefield and we'll be there to help you." You are dazed by the zoomorphic, anthropomorphic characters who are now trotting faster and faster past you and disappear into a tunnel ahead. You have so many questions, so you run after them, but you wake up from the dream and are left wondering whether to take any of it seriously. *It's just a dream*, you say to yourself. *A bloody dream.*

Early evening, a convoy of flying cars escort you to the shores of Mutirikwi, and as you arrive, a loud siren fills the atmosphere. "Oh-oh!" Garisanai's face displays not only horror, but urgency. "Our dome is down, and we're under attack! The siren only sounds when a virus attacks our systems at the research centre. This means we've been hacked, and the Mhondo-bots are deactivated. We're extremely vulnerable!"

"Quick, we have to find a SaNgoma to beat the *ngoma* so that Mwari can reprogramme the Dzim-AI!" Garisanai shouts, and you jump into one of the cars with her. You speed off towards the Great Enclosure where Ngoma Inoti Ngundu floats above the Conical Tower.

Above you, colossal airships covered with indecipherable Zhingoz orthography begin to release tanks and artillery across the terrain in all directions, from Topola to Nemamwa. They rumble into local villages, shooting and firing explosions, and chaos ensues. The serene flamboyant landscape of Dzimbabgwe is suddenly covered in acrid smoke. The cries of women and children punctuate the cracks of gunfire contaminating the atmosphere. Large wagons scoop precious stones and head for the Eastern borders where the stones of Dzimbabgwe will be shipped to the land of Zhingoz.

You arrive at the fortress entrance to find four armed Zhingoz soldiers blocking the road. "We must fight these idiots. Dzimbabgwe will never be colonised again!" Garisanai shrieks and you join her, charging towards the unsuspecting men. You fly-kick two of them at once and Garisanai finishes them off with her fists. You both disarm the Zhingoz and shoot them dead before speeding off to the SaNgomas' quarters about a kilometre away, where you find half of them have been shot and are writhing on the ground.

"Quick, we've got to save them!"

"Hurry! We're losing him!"

"She's not going to make it!"

"Oh my God, they've killed so many children!"

Amid the desolation, first aid is administered to injured civilians, and men and women are handed arms retrieved from hidden stores to fight back.

"Pfuko yaKuvanji! Pfuko yaKuuuvaaanjiiii!" You scream for help. The cacophony of war is deafening, can your voice be heard? Shrapnel flies in all directions, and within that racket, you spot a white maneless lion, with your pottery friends beside it. Zhingoz soldiers begin to fall mysteriously to their death, and you escape the scene with three SaNgomas, headed on foot to the Great Enclosure, a few hundred metres away. You are relieved that the dry-stone revetment walls are still intact.

A SaNgoma chants the sacred words to bring the *ngoma* down.

Our precious ngoma
Our rhythm of life
May you descend and
Release the sacred sound
The voice of Mwari
Full of prudence—
Our breath of life

The other catches it and immediately begins to beat the *ngoma*. The third one signals you to make your plea.

"Mwari *baba*, we are under attack. Our AI system has been hacked and the whole kingdom is vulnerable. Please help us!" You say as boldly as you can, clapping your cupped hands the traditional Karanga way.

It is well, my children.
Your systems are fixed.
Go forth and clean up your land.

In that moment, the deafening roars of awakening Mhondo-bots engulf the ether, their wrath stronger than ever. Within an hour, the enemies are devoured, and the treasurable defecations become mountainous. Just like waking up from a bad dream, the war is over. Except, there are bodies to be buried, and your inauguration to happen.

The next day, the atmosphere is sullen as civilians of Dzimbabgwe come to terms with what transpired. The smell of dead flesh is here and there, and everywhere. A mass funeral takes place, then you, Garisanai, and the wise counsel agree that the kingdom cannot carry on without an official custodian of the *ngoma*.

That evening, a convoy of vehicles escort you to the shores of Lake Mutirikwi, to witness your capture of the crocodile.

The air is laden with the sound of crickets and cicadas chorusing in harmony with croaking frogs and snorting hippos.

You're dressed in a tailor-made crocodile costume, to attract your target. You drag a large chunk of rancid donkey meat from a metal pail and throw it to the edge of the water, then lie on your stomach. In a few minutes, you spot a train of erect scutes meandering towards you in the water. Your noose is ready! A blanket is at hand!

The submerged ancient lizard lunges forward with its jaws wide open, rows of razor-sharp teeth glistening beneath the majestic moonlight. With lightning speed, it reaches for the donkey meat and clamps its jaws shut to drag it down. You jump onto its back and throw the blanket over its eyes, then quickly duct tape it securely around its face. The six-metre beast begins to spin forcefully, grunting viciously, its tail ready to rip anything in its way. You swiftly disembark and throw the noose over its mouth then drag the crocodile to the shore. Wild cheers of triumph and whistles grace the air.

"I got him!"

Young scientists from Mutirikwi Research Centre await, with sharp apparatus to cut up the aquatic beast.

"Wow! This one's got to weigh around 700 kilograms!" One of them marvels. "How on earth did you manage this?"

"I was trained for the job!" You wink at her. "To conserve the species, I've decided to not kill it. I think catching the crocodile proves beyond doubt that I can kill it. What we'll do to comply with *chivanhu* and complete the necessary rituals, is a keyhole operation to retrieve the gemstones in its stomach and sew it back. A part of its tail will be extracted to make the traditional inauguration meal. The crocodile will be kept at Mutirikwi Research Centre where it'll be nursed with broad-spectrum antibiotics until it's well enough to be returned into the lake."

Jubilation engulfs the air, and you know, you are home.

***

"Hey, are you ok? Sit up straight and take these for me my darling." Your eyelids part with anxious reluctance to find Nurse Helen doing her evening round of meds. "Ooof, it stinks in here! Have you soiled yourself again, my lovely? Never mind, I'll sort you out." The thirty-something old nurse busies herself and…*hang on a minute…*

"What time's my inauguration please?"

"Come again sweetie?" The patronising bitch is at it again. You can't stand it when she does this. The love bite you gave her is healing nicely, but you'll neck her again if she carries on like this.

"My fucken party, woman! When is it? Have you cooked the crocodile tail yet? Where are the stones!"

"What stones? There are no crocodiles in Herefordshire, darling!"

"The rubies and diamonds, mate! The gemstones! From the crocodile!"

"What?" Helen's getting close. She's going to push you down, isn't she? You'll bite her again if she gets any closer.

"No! You need to let me go or I'll miss my inauguration. Dzimbabgwe needs me!" You're getting out of bed to pack your things.

"I need back up!" Helen calls her people on the walkie-talkie. *For fucks' sake!*

"Traitor!" You spit at her. The PPE-kitted response team storms into your room within seconds to hold you down. "Leave me alone you fucken cunts! Don't touch me! I'll kick your ass! I can't breathe…" You scoop your shit and scatter it in all directions like seeds of mimosa touch-me-nots. You elbow and kick, and they increase in numbers.

"Shit! Get her into prone position!"

"Calm down Zorodzai!"

"Ok darling, you're safe here."

You're on your stomach on the bed and can barely move, but you lift your head, resisting still.

"Who the hell is Zorodzai? I am Murenga! Do you hear me? Don't fuck with my Nyabinghi energy…get the *hakata* engraved, bitches! I caught the crocodile!" Your pillow falls from the bed to the sparkling, white-tiled floor. The pills you should have been swallowing but kept under your tongue until the coast was clear…well, they follow the pillow and bounce onto the floor in slow motion, loudly spreading like spilled dried beans.

"Right, administer 10mg of Diazepam and 2mg Haloperidol!" Within seconds, they sink a large needle into your upper right butt cheek.

"Ouch! You're hurting me!" and another drill beneath the first one.

"I'm sorry, love…"

"Aargh! Mhondo-bots! Come and get these vile people! Mhondo-o-o-oooo!" You remain in combat mode.

"Alright, darling. Calm down…"

"Mhondo-bots! The colonisers are back! Oh no…you haven't hacked the Dzim-AI, have you? You and the Zhingoz are peas in a pod, aren't you? Aren't you!" Their poison courses through your veins, and you feel it sapping your willpower.

"That's it… That's a good girl. Let's get you cleaned up. James will be here soon. You've been dying to see him, haven't you?'

"Grandad James? He died a long time ago when Nana Mudavose left him for Dzimbabgwe. Is a ghost coming to visit me?" You're sweating. You're tired. Your huffs and puffs are laboured, and you're losing energy. This feels too familiar; you don't want to die again.

The weather carries your rage, rain falling in torrents as brilliant flashes of lightning bolt through your room. This is complemented by dramatic percussions of thunder resonating through the atmosphere. The dreaded signpost outside your window is blurred by the deluge, but its letters stare back at you, crystal clear: **St. Ethelwald's Psychiatric Unit.**

Glossary

Prologue

1. *Bute rematare* – cooked snuff

2. *Chapungu* - bateleur eagle

3. *Chisi* - day of rest

4. *Chivanhu* - traditional rituals

5. *Gwendengwe* - a revered spiritual being

6. *Hakata* - diviner's instrument

7. *Hungwe* - fish eagle

8. *Mhondoro* - lion spirit

9. *Mhotsi* – dreadlocks

10. *Mutovhoti* – African Sandalwood

11. *Njuzu* - mermaid

Weeping Tomato

1. *Ah, waidombovavo drangad* – Ah, so even you have been a drunkard also?

2. *Amapiano* – A genre of South African music, derived from House and Kwaito music

3. *Anodhliwa here maruva awo?* – can the flowers be eaten? / are those flowers edible? (implying that a plant that is not a source of nutrition is valueless / not worth talking about)

4. *bhabharasi* – hangover

5. *bhodho* – a large cast iron pot / sadza made in a large cast iron pot

6. *chema* – money offered to the bereaved, to help with funeral costs

7. *Chimbondisofta sha* – please soften me

8. *chikomba* – male lover

9. *chiuya mudiwa wangu* – come my love

10. *Eish! Ngaisiye matambo horaiti. Chete ndinobva ku*ghetto *kune ma*elders – Ok, let's leave it. It's just that I come from the ghetto where there are elders (who advise the young).

11. *fanika nezvawakaita iwewe so, handitundi* – with the way you are, I will not ejaculate

12. *Gombarume harina mwana* – a male lover owns no child – a Shona proverb meaning even if a lover impregnates a married woman, the child belongs to the man who paid bride price for the woman.

13. *Gomera uripo* – groan in situ / stay there and put up with it

14. *Haaa zvechingochani bodo zve* – no to homosexuality

15. *Ha mazita eikokovo* – Gosh, some of the names over there

16. *Haiwavo* – whatever / nonsense

17. *handirevi nhema* – I don't tell lies

18. *Hanti chero ku*church they burn incense? – even at church they burn incense, don't they?

19. *Hauchada Here* – You no longer want? (A song by Leonard Zhakata)

20. *Hino zvohumwi?* – So how can we resolve that? (A rhetorical question meaning there's not much we can do about that)

21. *Ini ndinobgwaira* – Me, I am blinking (literal translation) / I am well.

22. *Iwe dako iwe! Uripiko?* – You ass, where are you?

23. *Ko izvozvo wazviwanepi?* – Where did you get that idea from?

24. *Kungohwa hwi rako so, yodomira* – when I hear your voice, I get an erection

25. *Kurova guva* – beating the grave

26. *kwa*Mucheke *kwako ikoko* – over there in your Mucheke

27. *Makadiiko Mukanya?* – How are you Mukanya? (Mukanya is a Shona praise name for the monkey totem)

28. *Mangoma* – dancehall beats/music

29. *Ma small small awo* – that's a small issue (slang)

30. *Mbwende* – coward (song by Jah Prayzah)

31. *Mhaka dzaani?* – Who's fault is that?

32. *mhani* – word used to emphasise a point

33. *mudiwa* – loved one / my love

34. *mugaiwa* – sadza made from unrefined mealie-meal

35. *muna* - in

36. *muthi* – traditional medicines

37. *muri wezhira* – you're of the road (an idiomatic way of saying, you're from Masvingo)

38. *muzukuru* – niece/nephew/grandchild

39. *mwana wevhu* – child of the soil

40. Mweya Yerima – Dark Spirits (a song by Zimbabwean musician, Soul Jah Love)

41. *Ndaitaura sendine mishonga mukanwa, ukawanza shamwari, uchaaandiramba rimwe zuva. Hona, zvaitika… Ndaitaura sendinopenga,*

ukawanza shamwari, uchandiramba rimwe zuva. Hona, nhasi, zvaitika – I used to speak as if I had a magic potion in my mouth, saying too many friends will make you dump me one day. Look, it has happened. I used to speak like I was crazy, saying too many friends will make you dump me one day. Look, today it has happened.

42. *Ndatombotamba ipapa –* I actually danced a bit

43. *Ndezvekumama izvo –* that is shit

44. *ndinokuda –* I love you

45. *Ndinokuda nemoyo wangu wose –* I love you with all my heart

46. *Ndokuda wakadero –* I love you as you are

47. *Ndoda kuti uve wangu iwe –* I want you to be mine

48. *Nokuti gare gare tofa, saka kana ndodhla imbwa, ndododhla iri honho, kana zviri zvimbwanana ndoodhla zviri* two two! – Because after a while we die, so when I eat a dog, I'll eat a male one, and if they are puppies, I'll eat two at a time.

49. *Ndorevesazve! –* I'm telling you the truth!

50. *ndifonere ndimboku softa –* call me so I can soften you

51. *Nhema dzako! –* you lie!

52. *Nyangwe newevo –* so are you

53. *nzembe yangu yatorwa naaaniko? Ndatsvaka mudendere mayo ndaishayaaaaaa! –* who has taken my dove? I've looked for it in its nest and it is not there!

54. *Nzungu Ndamenya –* I have shelled the peanuts (a song by Zimbabwean musician Leonard Dembo)

55. *Pane varume vose pasi pano, hakuna anokuda seni mudiwa wangu. Zvose pasi nokudenga, hakuna wandoda kudarika iwe. Aiwa hakuna!* – Out of all the men in this world, none of them can ever love you the way I do. Both here on earth and in heaven, there's no one I love more than you. No, there is not!

56. *Sadza nenyama* – thick mealie-meal porridge and meat

57. *sungura* – a genre of Zimbabwean music

58. *Tibvigwe* – get away

59. *Unoziva chose dhali ndinovimba newe. Moyo wangu bhebhi urere pauri. Dhali, sei kundiita standby? Kundibata senge sipeyawiri. Bhebhi, ini ndave kushandura pfungwa dzanguuuuuu* – You know very well darling I trust in you. My whole heart baby, rests upon you. Darling, why would you place me on standby? Treating me like a spare wheel. Baby, I think I better change my mind.

60. *Uri mbgwa yemunhu* – you're a dog

61. *Unoda kungoita zvechihure chete?* – So you're only interested in whoring?

62. *Ubuntu* – I am what I am because of who we all are (humanity to others)

63. *wangu* – my person

64. *Zvizukuru zvaShaka zvizegwe vuno* – Shaka's grandchildren/descendants (beautiful women) are in abundance here

65. *zvomboreveiko?* – what does it actually mean?

66. *zvorevei?* – what does it mean?

The return of Mudavose

1. *bira* - all night ritual party to communicate with ancestors

2. *bute rehondo - raw snuff*

3. *bhosvo* - an antelope horn wind instrument

4. *chamupupuri* - whirlwind

5. *Chaminuka ndimambo, Ahe ndimambo, Shumba inogara yoga musango*
   - Chaminuka is king, yes he is king, a lion that lives on its own in the wild

6. *chokubata* - something to hold on to and live by

7. *hosho* - hand rattles

8. *hunhu* - being principled / noble

9. *kwazuvai* - greetings

10. *Kwazivai Tovera mudzimu dzoka! Haiwaiwa hoyiye mudzimu dzoka!* -
    Greetings Tovera our ancestor come back to us, (scatting) our ancestor
    come back to us

11. *makhadzi* - Tshivenda word meaning an aunt / father's sister, an integral
    family member

12. *makombgwe enyika* - spirit guides of a particular country

13. *makwa* - rhythmic hand clapping

14. *Mbakumba* - traditional Zimbabwean rhythm / dance, popular among
    the Karanga people

15. *mbira* - thumb piano

16. *Mhande* - traditional Zimbabwean rhythm / dance, popular among the
    Karanga people

17. *mhondoro* - spirit guide of a particular clan / lions

18. *mhoro* - hello

19. *murarabungu* - rainbow

20. *ndini* - I am

21. *Ngoma Inoti Ngundu* - the drum that goes ngundu

22. *nhare* - a type of mbira or thumb piano that communicates with ancestors in the otherworld

23. *nhekwe* - snuff container

24. *Nyamavhuvhu* - August

25. *nyikadzimu* - the dwelling place of ancestors

26. *vaera shava* - the eland totem clan

27. *vaera shoko* - the monkey totem clan

28. *Vana vanogwara. mudzimu dzoka!* - The children are sick our ancestor come back to us and help us

29. *vana vevhu* - children of the soil

Epilogue

1. *Zvine chirevo* - there is a deeper meaning to this

Acknowledgements

The inspiration for this novel took root when I was awarded a scholarship by Lolwe Academy in 2023 to attend their Magical Realism and Surrealism course, taught by the esteemed magical realism author, TJ Benson. During the course, I wrote several related short stories, which, after reviewing, TJ Benson remarked in our final class, "You have a compelling narrative voice that pulls a reader into your work… This reads like a 3rd or 4th novel… I think you are a novelist pretending to be a short story writer." His words struck a chord, prompting me to weave together some of my speculative fiction stories into a composite novel, which, after several rewritings, became Weeping Tomato. I'm deeply grateful to Lolwe Academy and TJ Benson for setting me on the path that led to this book.

The historical and mythological elements within this story are enriched by conversations with my father, a staunch pan-Africanist. In March 2024, I travelled from Wales to Masvingo to celebrate what would be his last birthday and shared with him the story of Weeping Tomato. He listened with delight, asking insightful questions, and offering invaluable information that guided my final research at the Great Zimbabwe Museum. His parting words to me, as I embraced him for the last time, were, "Never stop writing…". My father passed away unexpectedly in June 2024, and I dedicate this work to his memory; may his soul rest in peace. I am forever indebted to him for the wisdom he imparted to me.

A special thank you to Lazarus Panashe Nyagwambo and Innocent Whande, my wonderful editors who navigated this uncharted journey with me, bringing patience and grace to every step.

To my friends and family who beta read my manuscript at various stages of development, including Marian Christie for critiquing the poems— thank you for your invaluable feedback and support.

To the creatives who read and praised my book: Shingai Shoniwa, Shingi Mavima, Memory Chirere, Tariro Ndoro, Jon Lunn, and Mike Stuart— thank you for being amazing.

Mike Stuart, I cannot thank you enough for creating the beautiful interior and exterior visual artworks that bring this book to life.

Daniel Mutendi, your precision in laying out the story and poems, ensuring that every line, verse, shape, and dot is just so, has made all the difference— I sincerely appreciate you.

To my husband and children, my alpha readers, I am ever grateful for your unending love, patience, and encouragement of my creative endeavours.

Lastly, I offer my utmost gratitude to Mwari for guiding me in all that I do. It is through Her divine grace that the gift of writing flows within me.

About the author

Samantha Rumbidzai Vazhure is a British-born Zimbabwean bilingual author and visual artist who resides in Wales. She spent her childhood in Masvingo, Zimbabwe where she completed her education at Victoria Primary School and Victoria High School respectively. She returned to the United Kingdom in 1999 after completing her A Levels. She studied Law and Business Administration at the University of Kent in Canterbury and proceeded to study a Postgraduate Diploma in European Politics, Business and Law at the University of Surrey. Samantha works as a regulatory consultant in financial services.

Other works by this author:

1. *Zvadzugwa Musango* – a collection of poems exploring African womanhood in the context of displacement, penned in chiKaranga, a Shona dialect from Zimbabwe.

2. *Uprooted* – poems from 'Zvadzugwa Musango' translated to English.

3. *Painting a Mirage* – A debut novel and the first part of a trilogy, *The Mire*. The UK-born protagonist is raised in a privileged dysfunctional Zimbabwean family, then returns to live in the UK at the age of 18. Ruva, the protagonist, yearns to escape her toxic childhood, but relocation to the UK invokes a bitter confrontation with her illusionary upbringing; and she realises that she does not need to continue conforming to the dictates of her past. As Ruva navigates life in the UK as a first-generation immigrant, she begins to understand what it means to be a black minority living in a meritocracy. During her journey of learning to live independently, Ruva stumbles into marriage. Will the grass that seemed greener live up to her expectations?

4. 'Barcode' – a thriller highlighting the harsh truths of being an illegal immigrant in the UK. This short story is published in *Brilliance of Hope*, an anthology of short stories.

5. 'Tariro' – a piece of social commentary presented as a novelette. The urgency created by the protagonist's dilemma invites the reader's curiosity to how it is resolved. Hardships, alongside the themes of inequality, toxic religiosity, harassment, and bleakness of the patriarchal system, amongst others, are masterfully woven into a well thought out narrative. Also published in *Brilliance of Hope*.

6. *Turquoise Dreams* – An anthology of 29 short stories written by 10 Zimbabwean women, compiled and edited by Samantha Rumbidzai Vazhure.

7. *Brilliance of Hope* – An anthology of 41 short stories about the Zimbabwean dispersion, written by 15 Zimbabweans across the globe, compiled and edited by Samantha Rumbidzai Vazhure.

8. *Starfish Blossoms* – collection of poems where the reader is invited to discover the rich world of African womanhood. With meticulous structure and vivid detail, Starfish Blossoms explores the vagaries of patriarchy and women's hard-won victories, amid the abstractions of love, growth and death. This book won the National Arts Merit Award for Outstanding Poetry Book (Zimbabwe), in 2023.

9. *Tesserae: A mosaic of poems by Zimbabwean women* – An anthology of 174 poems by 37 women, co-compiled and edited with Marian Christie. The work is a unique celebration of Zimbabwean womanhood in all its diversity, its richness of voice and theme and narrative. The contributors include traditional page poets and underground poets, students and grandmothers, visual poets and spoken word artists, established writers and emerging talents, from within Zimbabwe and from the diaspora. *Tesserae* was voted one of 100 Notable African Books of 2023 by Brittle Paper.

10. *Pazvava Paipa* – An anthology of poems by 20 Zimbabwean poets in diverse dialects of the Shona language, compiled and edited by Samantha Rumbidzai Vazhure and Tanaka Chidora. The contributors include seasoned and emerging poets based in Zimbabwe and the diaspora.

11. Samantha's poetry and visual art appears in Ipikai Poetry Journal at www.ipikai.org and various anthologies such as *Once Upon No Time* by Empoweress Press, *Writing Woman Anthology - An Anthology of African Asian Writers and Artists Volume 3* by Mwanaka Media and Publishing Pvt Ltd., and *Zanna Zine* by We Are Zanna.

12. As editor and publisher, Samantha has published various works by Zimbabwean authors at www.carnelianheartpublishing.co.uk. She was voted African publisher of the year in 2023 by Brittle Paper as part of their Literary Person of the year Awards – an accolade that recognises individuals who have done outstanding work in advancing African literary culture and industry in the given year.